'Hypocrisy?' Gabriella echoed faintly.

'I dislike females who are scarcely out of the nursery, yet feel compelled to pass judgement on other people's failings,' Rick went on remorselessly. 'And at the same time suppress their own needs and desires...'

'I have no idea what you're talking about...'

'I'm tempted to kiss you, *ma petite*, to prove the point.'

'Just try it!'

'That's a dare that is too tempting to ignore!' Rick murmured, his voice thickening.

Dear Reader

With the worst of winter now over, are your thoughts turning to your summer holiday? But for those months in between, why not let Mills & Boon transport you to another world? This month, there's so much to choose from—bask in the magic of Mauritius or perhaps you'd prefer Paris...an ideal city for lovers! Alternatively, maybe you'd enjoy a seductive Spanish hero—featured in one of our latest Euromances and sure to set every heart pounding just that little bit faster!

The Editor

Having abandoned her first intended career for marriage, **Rosalie Ash** spent several years as a bilingual personal assistant to the managing director of a leisure group. She now lives in Warwickshire with her husband, and daughters Kate and Abby, and her lifelong enjoyment of writing has led to her career as a novelist. Her interests include languages, travel and research for her books, reading, and visits to the Royal Shakespeare Theatre in nearby Stratford-upon-Avon. Other pleasures include swimming, yoga and country walks.

Recent titles by the same author:

CALYPSO'S ISLAND
ORIGINAL SIN

AN IMPORTED WIFE

BY
ROSALIE ASH

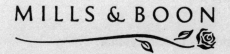

MILLS & BOON LIMITED
ETON HOUSE, 18-24 PARADISE ROAD
RICHMOND, SURREY TW9 1SR

*First published in Great Britain 1994
by Mills & Boon Limited*

© Rosalie Ash 1994

*Australian copyright 1994
Philippine copyright 1994
This edition 1994*

ISBN 0 263 78489 4

*Set in Times Roman 11½ on 12 pt.
01-9405-44343 C*

Made and printed in Great Britain

CHAPTER ONE

THE tall, dark, powerful-looking man, in sunglasses, khaki shirt and dusty cream trousers, seemed to be attracting attention, like bees to a honeypot. A willing porter scurried after him with his luggage, and another was practically breaking his neck to hail him a taxi as quickly as possible.

Lesser mortals, reflected Gabriella wryly, from her hot and dusty vantage point as she waited in the sun for a taxi for herself, could only look on, in envy and admiration.

She shifted position, waiting beside her suitcase, perspiration trickling uncomfortably down between her breasts, and dampening her jade T-shirt beneath the light white cotton jacket she wore. January in Mauritius, a tiny dot of an island far south in the vast expanse of Indian Ocean between Africa and Australia, was an abrupt contrast to January in London. Back home, she'd locked up her small one-bedroomed flat in Wimbledon and left behind icy sleet showers, and temperatures of minus two. Here, outside Plaisance Airport, the sun scorched down from a limpid blue sky, edged with fluffy tropical clouds, and it had to be at least ninety-five in the shade.

She lifted the heavy rope of honey-blonde hair at her nape, and blew upwards to cool her hot forehead. The tall man had been ushered respectfully into a taxi now, his cases stowed in the boot. She wouldn't have been surprised to see the porters bow and salute, as the taxi revved up to pull away.

It was hard to tell, behind his dark glasses, but she thought he was looking at her. She dropped her eyes quickly, hoping he hadn't had the satisfaction of seeing her gazing at him. In spite of her current aversion to the opposite sex, she had to concede that he looked disturbingly attractive. In fact, even from a safe distance, he was the most attractive man she'd ever set eyes on in her life, she acknowledged, a small twist of apprehension stirring her stomach. He looked lean, athletic, smooth-muscled. The dark brown hair, straight and thick, looked vibrantly clean and glossy, the wide, hard mouth, and the suggestion of five o'clock shadow on the firm jaw eye-catchingly male.

Strange, then, that he should remind her of Piers... Piers was blond, while this man was dark. Facially they weren't remotely similar. Piers was much younger, only twenty-five, whereas this man had an air of experience and sophistication that suggested early thirties. She identified the similarity, a subtle one. It must be that aura of

inborn privilege and careless arrogance which was
so reminiscent of Piers. The cool way he took all
the fuss and attention as his due...

She . unconsciously lifted her shoulders,
shrugging off the memories. It didn't matter any
more. About her disillusionment over Piers. Men
were definitely going to take a back seat in her
life from now on. Her career was showing signs
of progression. *That* was all that mattered. She
was new to this job, and she wanted to do well,
and on top of that she was here alone in advance
of the others. She should have been ac-
companying the fashion editor, who'd gone down
with the flu which had been decimating the entire
fashion department, literally at the eleventh
hour...

Now was her chance to prove herself, show
First Flair magazine that she was more than just
a lowly assistant. Until suitably experienced re-
inforcements could be dispatched, the responsibility for advance checking of locations for the
forthcoming fashion shoot lay on her novice
shoulders. It was exciting, and rather terrifying...

'Welcome to the Hotel Sable Royale,' smiled
a receptionist, when Gabriella finally presented
herself and her luggage. 'Did you have a good
journey, Madame Taylor?'

'Fine, thanks...' Apart from paying what
appeared to be a small fortune in *rupees* to the
taxi driver who'd just roared away from the
hotel entrance...

'But I'm not Madame Taylor...' Gabriella added, smiling apologetically. 'The rooms are booked in Ursula Taylor's name. But I'm Gabriella Howard, Mrs Taylor's assistant. Mrs Taylor was too ill to fly out with me...'

The pretty Creole girl shrugged and smiled again.

'OK. I hope you have a wonderful stay.'

She would, Gabriella reflected, following the porter carrying her suitcase to her room, if she could manage to fulfil her obligations to *First Flair* without any hitches, and, more immediately, if she could just cool off...

When the door was closed, she wasted no time, ripping off her jacket, sweat-damp jade T-shirt and smart jade culotte-skirt, tossing her coffee silk bra and pants on to the haphazard heap on the floor, twisting and pinning her blonde plait into a tight topknot, then running a cool shower in the elegant *en-suite* bathroom, and diving under it with relish.

The room which Ursula Taylor, *First Flair*'s stylish, thirty-something fashion editor, had apparently booked for her, was delightful, furnished in colonial style, with lots of wood and brass. A large balcony overlooked a crystal-white coral beach, fringed with soft, frondy pine trees. Beyond, a mill-pond-calm ocean glittered in the sun, turquoise and kingfisher-blue in its sheltering bracelet of coral reef.

Feeling slightly guilty, enjoying all this unbelievable luxury alone, while her boss languished
in London with a high fever, Gabriella emerged
from her shower, dried herself and found a baggy
white over-sized 'Minnie Mouse' T-shirt to pull
on while she searched for her hairdrier.

She was in the act of rummaging through her
flight-bag, for the travel-plug, when without
warning there was a hard hammering on the
bedroom door, and it was pushed forcefully open.
She leapt to her feet, her heart doing a shocked,
frightened somersault as the man who barged
furiously inside began with, 'Ursula, just what
the devil did you think you were playing
at——?' The gravel baritone clipped off abruptly
in mid-sentence. The confrontational anger
slowly died from his eyes, replaced by a wary
gleam of humour as he realised his mistake.

Hugging her arms around herself indignantly,
Gabriella found herself gazing up at the tall, dark
man in the khaki shirt and cream trousers whom
she'd been surreptitiously watching outside the
airport.

'I think I should be asking *you* that question,'
she heard herself saying, in a voice which
trembled uncontrollably. Something in the
darkness of his eyes was giving her unwelcome
shivers of awareness, all over her body.

Seeing him at closer quarters, she had a nig-
gling feeling she *had* seen this man somewhere
before... apart from outside the airport on her

arrival. His face was strangely familiar. Obviously he was someone Ursula knew...

Something she'd overheard in the office a couple of weeks ago darted back into her mind. Some gossip over problems in Ursula Taylor's marriage. Could this be Mr Taylor, pursuing his wife for a dramatic, romantic reconciliation? He was in his early thirties, about the same age as the woman she worked for...

'Do you make a habit of barging unannounced into other people's hotel rooms?' she added, her throat annoyingly dry.

The hard mouth twitched. But he was regarding her shocked expression and wide green eyes with grave apology.

'*Mille pardons*, if I have frightened you, *mademoiselle*. The door was not locked. I believed Madame Taylor to be in this room. So who are you?'

He was subjecting her to a cool, unhurried scrutiny, the gleam of male assessment making her inwardly wince.

'I am Ursula Taylor's assistant,' she said stiffly; 'Madame—er—Mrs Taylor has the flu. But you're...I mean, you're not Mrs Taylor's husband?'

'No.' The gravel-deep voice was wry as understanding dawned. 'I am not Mrs Taylor's husband.'

'Oh, I see...!' She tried her best, but it was quite impossible for her to keep the note of shocked dismay, even distaste, from her voice. This man wasn't too thick-skinned to be aware of it, even if he was insensitive enough just to loll there against the door-jamb, watching the emotions flitting across her face, instead of making a hasty, ashamed exit...

She bit her lip. She could only thank the gods she'd had time to put on the T-shirt. If he'd chosen to fling open the door a few seconds earlier, she'd have been stepping stark naked out of the shower. This man must have an intimate relationship with Ursula Taylor if he felt entitled to barge, unannounced, into her bedroom... Gabriella felt slightly sick, as the implications began to sink in. She might be naïve, but to her marriage was sacred. It didn't feel very pleasant to be caught up in the middle of what presumably could be an adulterous liaison...

He really seemed to have marked similarities to Piers, another of that cool, amoral breed who calmly disregarded convention, saw all women as fair game. But it took two to tango, as the saying went. What her married boss got up to in her private life was no business of hers, Gabriella reminded herself warily.

'I detect disapproval.' He shook his head sadly, mockery evident in every line of his face. 'You see me as a reckless philanderer, *mademoiselle*?' Amusement had deepened the voice still more. 'How refreshing to find someone still young enough to be shocked by the notion of extra-marital affairs. Truth comes from the mouths of babes and innocents, as they say.'

Colouring slightly, she gripped her arms more closely across her breasts, and fixed him with a level green gaze.

'*Philanderer* was your word, not mine. But if the cap fits...' she countered, with as much force as she could muster. 'And I assure you I'm neither a babe nor an innocent!'

'Ah. *Une vrai femme du monde*!' he teased gently. Deep-set eyes, unnervingly intense, moved probingly over her appearance, assessing her wet blonde hair, her slender figure, the long slim expanse of thigh, the mouse logo on the T-shirt. His eyes were an extraordinary colour. Not brown, not hazel, more a sort of molten, antique gold, Gabriella decided uneasily. Fringed with sable-dark lashes, and emphasised by the harshly cynical olive-skinned face, they were the most disconcerting eyes she'd ever encountered. 'A real woman of the world. How old are you, *mademoiselle*?'

'Twenty-one,' she supplied huskily. 'Old enough to know the score, Mr...?'

There was a brief pause, before he answered.

'Josephs. Rick Josephs.' The dark hand extended in greeting was large, lean, spatulate-fingered. She stared at it in panic for a split-second, before briefly, reluctantly shaking it. Rick Josephs didn't sound a very French name for a Frenchman. She assumed he was French, at any rate. He certainly spoke French, although when he spoke in English his French accent was negligible. A mystery hybrid, she decided dubiously. One of those global travellers with the panache and confidence to fit in anywhere...

'Gabriella Howard.' She whipped her hand away from his with unseemly speed. The warm strength of the hand-clasp was unbelievably disturbing. Glaring at him in a sudden, unexpected spurt of defensive fury, she added, 'Now that we're formally introduced, would you please *go*? As you see, Mrs Taylor is not hiding under the bed, or lurking behind the door. If you want to see her so urgently, you'll have to hop on the plane back to London and minister to her on her sick bed! Although *Mr* Taylor might be a bit surprised.'

A faint grin lit the dark face, as he absorbed her sudden outburst. 'It can wait,' he said briefly, straightening up from the doorway with infuriating lack of haste. 'Is Ursula still intending to fly out here when she's well?'

'Oh, yes. Along with half a dozen others! Meanwhile, by default, I'm the advance location scout for this fashion shoot...'

He paused at the door, his gaze narrowing. 'Are you indeed? I might be able to help you there.'

'I'm sure I can manage quite well without your help, thanks!' The sharp retort was out before she had time to analyse it.

The grin grew broader. 'I have to hand it to you, Mademoiselle Howard, you have spirit. High principles. A more timid employee might think twice about being rude to a friend of her boss. Might, perhaps, fear for her job?'

She stared at him, her heart suddenly beginning to pound at twice its normal speed. She was so angry that she could hardly find her voice, but his words had jolted her back to reality. He might be arrogant and patronising, and he might have barged into her room and narrowly missed catching her in an embarrassing state, but he evidently knew Ursula Taylor very well indeed. Even if he appeared to be enjoying taunting her over the mix-up, it wasn't her place to appear to be passing judgement on the situation.

She chewed her lip, in a turmoil of uncertainty. With a sudden surge of emotion, she found herself detesting the man, with an intensity which took her by surprise.

'What sort of a person *are* you?' she demanded shakily.

'The lowest and most despicable, *bien sûr*. But don't worry,' he teased, opening the door and observing her pink-cheeked fury with a short laugh, 'we philanderers are *very* discreet. *A bientôt, mademoiselle*.'

He'd gone. She found herself glaring helplessly at the closed door, unable to recall ever feeling such a violent loathing for someone she barely knew. *A bientôt?* She'd think herself lucky if she never had to see him again!

Her luck was out. Fierce hopes of avoiding bumping into him again evaporated as she walked out to the palm-tree-dotted poolside restaurant an hour later. He was drinking red wine, lazily relaxed on a bar stool, darkly attractive in a white dinner-jacket and an amber bow-tie which seemed to emphasise his golden eyes. Around him, in an animated group, milled several glamorous-looking people who appeared to be hanging on his every word. Two girls in particular held Gabriella's attention. Chic, dark, svelte as models, they fawned over him, vying for his attention. In clinging evening dresses, they looked dauntingly poised and beautiful. For a few seconds, Gabriella felt rooted to the spot, glancing round uncertainly at the other guests, standing near the bar or seated at the candlelit tables all around the circular floodlit pool.

Her heart plummeted. Everyone seemed to have dressed for dinner! Everywhere she looked she saw silks and crêpe de Chines, sequins and satins. And here she was, face bare of make-up, hair dragged into a high French plait, in a favourite but totally unsuitable short apple-green cotton T-shirt dress, and flip-flops...

Rick Josephs had seen her. Half turning from his seat on the bar stool, he raised a hand in brief salute, his eyes lingering on her for a while, his expression unreadable. The girls nearest him turned too, eyeing Gabriella with swift, derisive glances before swinging away, resuming their vivacious conversation.

Too late to duck back upstairs, and riffle through her skimpy wardrobe for her smartest dress. She'd look an immature idiot, if she ran out now. She'd just have to brazen it out.

Head high, she aimed for the bar and smiled confidently at the friendly Asian barman.

'I'd like a...a glass of pineapple juice, please...'

Near by, she could hear one of the girls and Rick Josephs talking in rapid French, his husky, amused baritone growl a contrast to her cool feminine voice. With relief, she realised that the head waiter had spotted her, and was bearing down on her, smiling in welcome.

'*Bonsoir*, Mademoiselle Howard. Would you like me to show you to your table?'

'Oh, yes. Thank you...' She followed him, averting her gaze as she passed Rick Josephs. As she drew level with his party, one of the girls in the group surrounding him burst into a peal of laughter, swirled blindly round, glass in hand, and collided head-on with Gabriella. With a gasp of dismay, Gabriella felt the contents of the glass of red wine splash down the front of her dress.

'Oh, *pardon*! I am so sorry...' The girl was definitely slightly tipsy. From the laughingly unrepentant expression on her face, as she eyed

Gabriella's casual outfit, she didn't view the accident with too much gravity.

Pink-faced, Gabriella stared down at the spreading stains on her dress, suddenly the centre of everyone's attention, wishing she could vanish into thin air.

'It doesn't matter...' Embarrassment engulfed her. Not only was she not dressed in an evening gown, as everyone else appeared to be, she was also sporting a T-shirt dress with red wine all over it...

'*Mademoiselle*, how unfortunate...' the head waiter was saying anxiously. 'Perhaps you would like to change your clothes before you sit down to dinner...?'

'Yes...I think I'd better...'

They were interrupted by Rick Josephs, who took charge of the situation with cool aplomb.

'Leave it to me, René,' he told the head waiter with a grin. 'Come with me, Gabriella...'

When he took her arm, she was so stunned by his audacity that she barely had time to argue before she was escorted away from the restaurant, and into the cicada-filled darkness of the hotel gardens.

'Let go of my arm,' she said, icily polite, swinging to confront him as he dropped his hand. 'You'd be far better off chatting up your *drunken* female admirers at the bar than hauling me out here...!'

He gave a weary sigh, eyeing her taut face with wry annoyance.

'Gabriella ... you don't mind if I call you Gabriella?'

'As a matter of fact, I do ...'

'You must try not to judge people so harshly,' he went on softly, ignoring her. 'I apologise for the accident, and for the clumsiness of my companion. And I will buy you a new dress.'

'I happened to like this one!' she countered obstinately, with what she knew to be a lamentable lack of social grace. 'And just because I have certain ... standards ... doesn't mean that I judge people harshly ...'

'*Dieu!*' he growled, half laughing and half angry, catching her by the shoulders and giving her a slight shake. 'What an unbearable little *prig* you are, Gabriella!'

His words seemed to hit her square in the face. Opening her mouth to retort, she felt her throat tighten without warning. Abruptly, her fragile poise began to crumble, and anger came to her rescue.

'I couldn't really care less about your opinion of me,' she retorted shakily, trying to free herself from his firmly guiding hand as he steered her through the undergrowth. 'I assure you my opinion of you is *every* bit as low! Where are we going ... ?'

'My mother taught me that to remove red wine the stain must be soaked in white wine,' he retorted calmly, 'as quickly as possible.' They'd reached a detached white villa, palms swaying beside the arched, carved wooden doorway, the air heavy with the lush musky scent of tropical flowers. 'Come inside, and take off your dress. I can supply the white wine, if you wish to put my mother's remedy to the test?'

The sardonic grin as he ushered her inside what seemed to be a private villa in the hotel grounds sent her temper soaring even higher.

'Take my dress off...? Are you *serious*?'

'Why, yes——' he spread his hands ironically '—unless you wish me to pour white wine over it while you are wearing it?'

'Look, if this is some kind of...of cheap seduction technique...'

'Far from it, Gabriella.' He was guiding her into a luxurious wood-panelled bathroom, handing her a grey Paisley silk robe before leaving her. 'You are not my type. I prefer older, *married* women. Or drunken pick-ups at hotel bars. Remember?'

Hot colour burned her cheeks as she stared at his mocking dark face. Catching an angry breath in her chest, she demanded unsteadily, 'And what am I supposed to wear to dinner, your silk dressing-gown?'

'Relax. I promise I will not let you starve.'

He withdrew, leaving her seething with mixed emotions, not least of which was acute apprehension.

After a long, indecisive wrestle with her temper, she rammed the bolt home on the door, and then slowly slid the apple-green dress off. She examined her white lacy bra. There was a red stain on that, too, but she'd rather die than present her underwear for Rick Josephs's stain-removing treatment.

With the Paisley robe belted tightly enough to endanger her circulation, she emerged with the dress.

Rick Josephs had discarded his white dinner-jacket, and loosened his bow-tie. He was stretched out quite happily on a white Lloyd-Loom-style cane chair on a paved balcony with a spectacular view of the moonlit ocean, as she came reluctantly in search of him.

When he saw her he stood up, took the dress from her stiff fingers, and waved an opened bottle of white wine with a lop-sided smile.

'OK. Now we marinate the dress in the white wine,' he quipped lightly, bearing it off into what looked to be an expensively equipped kitchen. 'Can I get you a drink?'

'I . . . no, thank you.'

He returned, minus the dress, but carrying a silver tray with a freshly opened bottle of wine, and two glasses.

'I said "no, thank you". Do you ply all your female acquaintances with alcohol?' she queried, sweetly sarcastic.

He paused in the act of pouring, one dark eyebrow raised quizzically.

'No. It is not always necessary,' he mocked obliquely. 'Usually my female acquaintances are quite happy to relax with me, without the aid of alcohol.'

Embarrassment heated her face again.

'How gratifying for you,' she smiled through gritted teeth. 'So what went wrong with your female friend at the bar?'

The golden gaze gleamed ominously. 'Sit down, Gabriella,' he suggested softly, pulling out one of the white cane chairs, and waiting with an air of patient confidence. 'Let's see if we can hold a civilised conversation while we are waiting for our dinner to arrive.'

'While . . . what?' The flustered feeling was intensifying. 'Our dinner?'

'We can eat here. Give us the perfect chance to get to know each other a little better. So that when Ursula gets here she can see what excellent friends we have become? *D'accord*?'

Mutinously, she glared at him. Why did she get the feeling that this was some subtle, teasing kind of blackmail?

She shivered a little, her hands clenched in the pockets of the silk robe. There was something about his sophisticated, world-weary manner which made her feel about twelve years old. And yet the dark glitter in his gaze made her feel quite

the opposite. Gabriella doubted if she'd ever felt
so bewildered by her own reactions...

In silence she sat down in the chair opposite
his, and crossed her legs. Equally silent, he finished pouring the wine, and handed her a glass.
As she reached to take it, the silky grey material
of the robe slithered stubbornly off her thighs,
and she hastily uncrossed her legs and tugged the
fabric back in place, clamping her knees together.
When she met Rick Josephs' enigmatic gaze
across the table, she saw that he was laughing at
her.

'Perhaps you have a low opinion of men in
general. But I assure you, I am not a sex-crazed
beast...' he mocked gently.

'Your private life is of no interest to me.' She
sounded stiffly pompous, she knew she did. Her
stomach was tight with tension as she warily
sipped her wine.

'So tell me, what is?' The lazy question caught
her by surprise. He was regarding her levelly over
his glass, his narrowed gaze unreadable. She
stared at him in blank silence for a while, then
slowly shook her head.

'I'm sorry...?'

'What interests you, Gabriella?'

'That's a rather sweeping question, isn't it?'
She frowned at him, doubting his sincerity. This
was another mocking wind-up, she was sure. 'I
suppose my job, at the moment.'

'So you are ambitious? At the moment, you are an assistant to a fashion editor. What are your ambitions within *First Flair* magazine?'

She shrugged, then laughed uncertainly. 'Whatever promotion comes along, I suppose. Although there have been rumours recently that there's a change of ownership on the cards for the magazine. So things may not be all that...stable. In the long term...'

She'd heard rumours, in fact, that Piers and his father had made a bid for the magazine. Which could no doubt spell an abrupt end to her career prospects in that particular environment. But it was no use worrying about it. She'd become philosophical lately. One day at a time...

'Are you well qualified?' He'd been watching her silent reverie with an amused expression.

'Reasonably well. I took a fashion design course at St Martin's, while I was working for a PR company. I've worked with fashion stylists, and that's really what I want to do—fashion styling...'

For the life of her, she couldn't fathom why he should be so interested in her career plans in the fashion world. Unless he was involved in it personally? That possibility had only just occurred to her. The glamorous girls at the bar had been tall and willowy and elegant enough to be models...

'Styling?' Rick had nodded, his expression deadpan. 'Are you any good at it?'

'I think so.'

'So that explains why they've trusted you to organise locations for this fashion shoot. You're in charge of the look, are you? The location, models, hair, make-up?'

'Well, only by default, as I told you. The others due to come out with me have been flattened by this flu virus. Do you work for *First Flair*?' she demanded suddenly, feeling even more confused. He seemed altogether far too knowledgeable about the whole business.

He shook his head, with a faint grin. 'No. Not exactly.'

'What kind of an answer is that? Not exactly? You're on intimate terms with Ursula Taylor, and you seem to know an awful lot about magazine fashion work...'

'I would describe myself as self-employed.'

'So what are you doing in Mauritius?'

'Relaxing, after some arduous power-play. I spend a lot of time here. I was born here.'

'You're Mauritian?'

He smiled. 'Franco-Mauritian. My ancestors settled here in the eighteenth century. A motley crew of pirates and corsairs, I regret to confess. Enticed here by the French East India Company to colonise the island...'

'Enticed?'

'They were enticed by offers of money, and land. And women. Girls were rounded up on the quaysides in France, and shipped out here to provide them with the means to procreate. The prospect of an ''imported wife'' must have been the deciding factor, don't you think?'

She blinked at the relentless gleam of mockery in his eyes.

'So... you don't actually *live* here?'

He shook his head. 'I live in New York. Or in Paris. Sometimes in London. But whenever I can, I come back here. I'm planning on having a house built here, at the moment.'

'I see.' She stared at him, frustrated by his subtle, deliberate evasiveness, her thoughts whirring uncontrollably. When a long silence had stretched out, he lifted a curious eyebrow.

'You look lost in thought, Gabriella.'

'I was thinking how your ancestry throws a lot of light on your character!' she heard herself saying coolly. 'When you're descended from a bunch of pirates, I expect a small matter of... *adultery* is of no importance at all...'

Instantly rather ashamed of her snide insult, she watched his face tauten slightly, darken with anger. Her heart jolted in her chest. Quickly standing up, she put her glass on the table, and turned away. 'Thanks for the drink. If you'll excuse me, I'd rather eat alone tonight...'

She got no further than the door. She found herself captured, trapped against it by at least six feet of lean masculinity. Her throat choked with anger and emotion, she glared up at him in alarm.

'Let me go...' she began shakily.

'In a moment.' She couldn't say he was exerting force, she reflected hazily, because he was hardly touching her. His hands were on the door, on either side of her, effectively imprisoning her without body contact. Likewise, his torso, smoothly muscled beneath the fine white lawn of his shirt, threatened to move closer but didn't, hovering alarmingly just an inch away from the agonised tips of her breasts. The moment was intimate but restrained.

'I'm a tolerant man,' he continued, huskily amused, 'but I am getting rather tired of being insulted, Miss Gabriella Howard.'

'Let me *go* . . .'

There was an elusive trace of expensive cologne, the clean, warm, musky smell of his body. Her senses whirled. She was close enough to see dilated black pupils in the centre of the golden irises, to notice the faint blue-black smudge of evening beard-growth along his chin. She should be feeling threatened, she reflected dazedly, but instead she felt overwhelmed with physical awareness. It was like someone pressing a switch, triggering a new set of emotions previously dormant . . .

'I dislike hypocrisy,' he added, as if she hadn't spoken.

The shadowed amber gaze moved up and down her trembling body, lingering deliberately on the points of her nipples beneath the Paisley, on the parted fullness of her mouth.

'Hypocrisy?' she echoed faintly.

With a hard smile, he stepped back a fraction, freeing her. She found that her knees had weakened to the point where she found it hard to move.

'I dislike females who are scarcely out of the nursery, yet feel compelled to pass judgement on other people's failings,' he went on remorselessly, watching as the colour came and went in her cheeks. 'And at the same time suppress their own needs and desires...'

'I have no idea what you're talking about...'

'Oh, yes, you have,' he grinned, reaching unexpectedly to capture her chin, tilting her face up for inspection. Their eyes met, and for a split-second, caught up in that magnetic golden gleam, Gabriella felt as if she was mentally slipping out of control. 'I'm tempted to kiss you, *ma petite*, to prove the point.'

'Just try it,' she flung at him, choking on her fury. 'I promise you'll regret it!'

He gave a low, impatient laugh, and caught hold of her shoulders, twisting her round to him.

'That's a dare that is too tempting to ignore!' he murmured, his voice thickening. Then he dropped his dark head to take slow, expert possession of her mouth.

CHAPTER TWO

IT WASN'T so much a kiss as a light, sensual caress of the lips. But while it lasted all comparisons between Piers and Rick Josephs vanished abruptly from Gabriella's mind. The feel of the hard male lips brushing tantalisingly over hers, the wave of reaction as the muscular body made contact with hers, was overpowering. Everything else simply melted from her consciousness. All she was capable of thinking was that, even if she'd once imagined she'd been in love with Piers, he'd never had this devastating physical effect on her.

This was something new, shockingly intense. Unthinkable...

Battling to her senses, rigid with denial, she summoned the will-power to push Rick fiercely away. The emotion he'd aroused in her had left her feeling weak and shaky, and very frightened by her own responses.

'If you've quite finished?' she said in a low, choked voice. 'Frankly, I need a lot more than a glass of white wine to stand being mauled by men like you!'

Rick Josephs' face was a mask of cool mockery.

'Next time I'll have champagne on ice,' he quipped with a bleak grin. 'Won't you stay and have dinner with me, Gabriella?'

'Not in a million years!' She grabbed the doorhandle, snatching it open. 'I'd rather starve ... !'

Uncaring of the Paisley robe, she escaped into the humid darkness and made her way, half walking, half running, towards the lights and laughter of the hotel.

No one seemed surprised to see her asking for her room key at Reception dressed in a man's silk robe. But she felt acutely embarrassed. Mortified, she finally made it back to her room, and slammed and locked the door behind her, almost numb with disbelief at the events of the evening so far, and her own emotional over-reaction to them.

She ought to ring Room Service, she supposed distractedly, order herself a snack in her room. The thought of going down to the restaurant again tonight was more than she could face. That hateful, mocking man ... with his glamorous girlfriends at the bar, and his suspicious relationship with her boss ...

Shivering, Gabriella went across to sit at the kidney-shaped dark wood dressing-table, gazing at her pale reflection in the oval mirror.

She touched her fingers slowly to her mouth. It hadn't even been a madly passionate kiss. There'd been no dramatic fencing of tongues or hungrily devouring attempts to reach her tonsils, the way Piers had favoured. Ironically enough, it had been rather a chaste kiss. So why had it left her feeling as if she'd been seduced by someone in the master class...?

The silk robe felt like a caress against her skin. With trembling fingers, she abruptly tore it off, and threw it angrily into the corner of the room. How she was going to return it she couldn't imagine. The thought of seeking him out for the purpose filled her with dread. Yet she could hardly hand it to Reception and ask them to return it to the man in the private villa. Not if she valued her reputation...

But then there was the small matter of her dress. Presumably, Rick Josephs would return that at some point. She could hand the robe back then. As quickly as possible. And then steer clear of him, as firmly as she could...

Blankly, she examined her face. Large sage-green eyes stared back, from a heart-shaped bone-structure strengthened by a firm, chisel-shaped chin. She was here in Mauritius to prove that she could do a good job, she reminded herself sternly. Preliminary set-backs such as these brief skirmishes with a man like Rick Josephs were trivial, and irrelevant.

Dragging her shattered defences together, she rinsed her face in the bathroom, then picked up the telephone and ordered a light salad to be sent up to her room. Food, a good night's sleep, and a strict veto on her wayward emotions. That was all she needed to set her back on course, surely?

Digging in her luggage, she found the thick historical paperback novel she'd begun on the plane, settled herself on her bed, and determinedly lost herself in the fictional world of the nineteenth century.

'Helicopter trips to surrounding islands?' The girl at Reception nodded doubtfully. 'Yes, it is possible. I will try to organise a trip for you...'

'Thanks.' Gabriella smiled hopefully. She was feeling a small glow of self-confidence returning this morning. She'd eaten a delicious breakfast, delivered to her room and consumed on her balcony with its breathtaking vista of ocean and beach. The warm rolls and exotic fruit juice and fragrant creamy coffee had done much to restore her equilibrium, even if she hadn't slept as well as normal. With her long blonde hair in a high, tight plait, flat tan sandals on bare feet, and in a short white cotton sundress, the cross-over backstraps allowing maximum air to circulate, she was bright and raring to go. She shifted the roomy raffia bag, containing money, camera, sun-lotion and all manner of other necessities, a little higher on her shoulder, and waited expectantly.

'The problem is the weather,' the girl was saying, shaking her head as she consulted with another member of the hotel staff. 'Regular trips around the islands are not running at the moment...'

'The weather?' Gabriella echoed, perplexed, glancing over her shoulder at the sapphire sky and dazzling sunshine. 'What's wrong with the weather?'

'Cyclones are forecast.'

Gabriella stared at the girl pleadingly.

'There's no sign of any cyclones yet,' she pointed out encouragingly. 'My boss in London rang this morning. She's very insistent that I take a look at Rodrigues as a potential location. There are some marvellous remote areas, with dramatic waterfalls and——'

'Not even the all-powerful Ursula Taylor can play God with the tropical weather, Gabriella.'

The deep voice was all too familiar. As she spun round, her heart sank. Rick Josephs lounged against the end of the reception desk, wickedly dark and handsome in sawn-off denims, espadrilles and a plain white T-shirt.

'Good morning,' she supplied briefly, shooting him a cool, repressive look. 'Do you never mind your own business?'

'Such gratitude. When I was about to offer my services as taxi driver?'

'*Taxi driver*?' She couldn't help her jaw dropping slightly.

'And guide,' he added calmly, exchanging an enigmatic smile with the girl receptionist, who was gazing at him as if he were royalty. 'Ignore

Ursula. There is no need to go five hundred kilo-
metres to search for locations on Rodrigues when
Mauritius has everything you need.'

'Oh, so I ignore my employer, do I?' she countered, feeling her temper rising all over again.
'Why do I get the feeling you're *trying* to get me
sacked?'

'Paranoia will not get you very far in the
fashion world, Gabriella.' He'd sauntered closer,
eyeing her appearance with casual interest. 'How
urgently do you need to explore for locations?'

'*Very* urgently,' she told him, resenting his
presence but struggling with her antagonism.

'Then since you'll find that all the commercial
helicopter operators will have shut up shop
pending this cyclone, my humble jeep and I are
available for hire,' he informed her, grinning at
her tightly set face. 'At a price to be agreed.'

'I'm sure *First Flair* would pay normal rates,'
she retorted stiffly. '*If* I took you up on the offer,
which is unlikely!'

'I'm sure Ursula would expect you to use your
common sense,' he purred smoothly. 'Make use
of any available help to facilitate the project.'

This was undoubtedly true. Damn the man.
She felt hopelessly inexperienced suddenly,
unsure how to handle the situation.

'Well, yes. But what about this cyclone?' She
glanced back at the receptionist, praying for some
other suggestion. 'How long before it comes? Is
it dangerous? Should I let *First Flair* know...?'

'Bad cyclones are quite rare,' Rick Josephs reassured her calmly. 'Normally they are just high winds and torrential rain, over quite quickly.'

'I see. Well, thanks for the offer, but I'm sure I can find some other means of transport...'

Torn between telling him to get lost, and possibly needing his help, she turned back to the receptionist, who'd been joined by the manager.

'If you are in a hurry to see different places, I suppose you could get a taxi, or hire a car yourself...' the manager began helpfully.

'No, she couldn't,' Rick put in calmly. 'The young lady is under age. Twenty-three's the minimum, isn't it?'

'Ah, yes, that is true... If Monsieur Josephs is prepared to help, he knows the island very well,' the manager confirmed. 'And I can vouch for his integrity. I'd say it seemed the perfect solution, *mademoiselle*...'

'Perfect,' said the lazy voice at her side.

Gabriella looked round, and found his golden eyes mockingly intent on her indecision. Heart thudding as the options sank in, she capitulated with a brief, angry shrug.

'Then I suppose I'm stuck with Monsieur Josephs,' she agreed sweetly.

'A wise decision, graciously made,' he applauded softly, taking her arm and escorting her out of the hotel. 'And may I say how delighted I am to be given the chance to spend more time in your charming company, Gabriella?'

'They say sarcasm is the *lowest* form of wit,' she reminded him, in a furious undertone.

'*Je m'excuse*,' he murmured unrepentantly, ushering her around to the car park of the hotel where a large open-topped jeep glinted in the sun. 'You seem to have the knack of bringing out the lowest traits in my character.'

'You have other traits?' She met his narrowed gaze with wide, unblinking eyes, and he burst out laughing.

'All right,' he said finally. 'If we are to spend the day together, perhaps we could agree on a truce.'

She chewed her lower lip, then looked away from him and sighed, feeling faintly ashamed of herself. 'You're right. I'm sorry. I suppose a spell of adult civility wouldn't hurt.'

'An apology? This is progress!' The smile he shot towards her as he fired the engine was infectious, and wickedly amused, she registered uneasily. Despite everything, she supposed he did have a few likeable qualities, but she'd be crazy to trust him. She knew very little about him, but she sensed he was a renegade. A descendant of those lawless pirates who'd first colonised the island . . . and he was too much like Piers . . .

'Did you say this was your jeep?' she managed in a determinedly civil tone of voice.

He nodded, his eyes now hidden behind dark glasses as he concentrated on the winding road up from the beach.

'Do you keep it at the hotel?'

'It's convenient, until my house is finished.'

'Where are you building your house?'

'On a small island off the coast.'

She found herself staring at him, speechless.

'A small island? A private island, you mean?' It was no good, she couldn't keep the spark of professional interest out of her voice.

'Private enough.' He glanced at her quizzically, his mouth twisting. 'I own it. Don't tell me. You think you could use it for your fashion shoot?'

'I didn't say that, but... is it easily accessible?' she countered cautiously. If Ursula Taylor knew this man so well, why hadn't she tipped Gabriella off about the possibility of a private island for the shoot? It would be ideal, surely...?

'It's a short trip by motorboat. But for today I had in mind a scenic tour of the whole island, Gabriella, starting with the Savanne region in the south...'

The message seemed definite. Steer clear of his private island. Gabriella subsided reluctantly, absorbing the scenery, trying not to brood on this intriguing revelation.

It was hot and humid. The heat of the sun was like a naked flame against her face as they drove. She pulled sunglasses and a small white cotton sunhat out of her bag and jammed them firmly in place. She had a long-sleeved shirt rolled up in her bag, in case the high protection sun-lotion she'd plastered on earlier ceased to feel protective. Notebook to hand, camera round her neck, keeping up a non-stop flow of questions, she twisted and turned in fascinated interest at the ever-changing scenery. There was sugar cane in waving green abundance along the sides of the road. Palm trees, fanning their tropical fronds against the cobalt sky. Grey-white monkeys with sweet, friendly faces crouched in the twisted branches of trees. Mountains with irregular twisted peaks coated in green. Above it all swirled sporadic clouds, fluffy and innocuous to Gabriella's mind.

This talk of cyclones seemed like unnecessary scaremongering . . .

'A low-altitude helicopter flight is the best way to see the island.' Rick glanced at her lit-up face, when she'd made an involuntary exclamation at the sight of a dramatic gorge, with tumbling water flowing seawards. 'If the weather had been more predictable, I'd have taken you up in the Jet Ranger. From the air, you can see how the landscape changes dramatically. . .'

Taken her up in the Jet Ranger? Was he saying he had his own private helicopter, too? Gabriella decided to stop speculating about this man, just go with the flow. It made no difference, anyway. She didn't like him, she didn't trust him, and, although she knew it was unfairly prejudiced on her part, with all his casual wealth and privilege

and power he was appearing more like Piers
Wellington by the second...

They lunched at a restaurant with a big, thatch-
roofed awning, and dramatic views over a
tranquil turquoise lagoon. Beyond the distant
coral reef, the Indian Ocean surged with om-
inous potency, and sprayed warning plumes of
white foam.

Gabriella, on her companion's advice, chose
palm-heart salad, with *pommes d'amour*, tiny
cherry tomatoes which Rick told her grew all over
the island, and then *camarones*, grilled fresh-
water prawns, followed by a small fresh pineapple. This had been peeled and cut into spirals,
with the stem left as a handle. By the end of the
meal she was feeling so relaxed that she was in
danger of forgetting her mission.

Across the table, Rick watched her with that
now familiar worldly, amused tolerance. He
paused in the act of biting into his pineapple, the
yellow juice running over his fingers.

'What did you think of the sacred Hindu lake,
the Grand Bassin?' he queried softly, watching
her licking the sweet, sugary juice off her own
lips. 'Suitable for your fashion shoot?'

'Hardly—somehow sacred lakes don't go with
flashy fashion articles, do they?'

He laughed. 'I'm not sure that's the attitude
for an ambitious fashion stylist, Gabriella. What
about the Botanical Gardens? The pond of lotus
flowers? The giant Amazon water lilies?'

She frowned reflectively.

'They were beautiful, but...' She'd loved the peaceful atmosphere there, the cooing of the pigeons, the lizards, the brilliant flashes of tropical birds. Rick had shown her a huge talipot palm tree, which flowered only once in its lifetime of sixty years, and then died in a glorious mass of yellow blooms...

She hesitated, reaching for the starched white linen napkin to wipe her fingers, then plunged in with what she'd had on her mind for the last hour or so. 'Before I draw up a shortlist, is there any chance we could take a look at this island of yours? I mean, if it's small and private, it would be absolutely ideal for *First Flair*'s purposes. We could do anything we liked, without fear of upsetting the locals...!'

'Sounds intriguing,' he teased. 'What did you have in mind? An open-air orgy?'

She coloured slightly. 'Don't be silly. But, well, obviously you wouldn't know anything about it, but with fashion shoots there can be an awful lot to organise and...'

He angled an eyebrow, gravely non-committal. 'Yes?'

'I'm sure *Ursula* would appreciate it if you helped us out!' she finished up, with a stroke of inspiration. 'In fact, I'm surprised she hasn't already suggested it!'

'Perhaps Ursula doesn't even know about it?' he suggested blandly.

Gabriella lowered the chunk of pineapple she'd been about to finish, and met his mocking gaze. He was leaning back in his chair, eyes narrowed, but his expression impossible to read. She felt a fresh jolt of annoyance. He was playing games with her. She sensed that strongly now. And the more frustrated and annoyed she became, the more he'd be quietly enjoying himself.

The only solution was to stay calm. And polite.

'All right, I'm sorry I asked,' she said evenly, 'And I do appreciate your help today. I'd never have known where to go without a knowledgeable guide...'

'Finish your lunch, and spare me the flowery gratitude, Gabriella,' he grinned. 'It makes me feel distinctly uneasy. We'll continue our coastal tour. Some of the finest beaches are along the next stretch.'

'Which coast does your island lie off?' She asked the question casually, as they walked slowly back through a shady belt of casuarinas towards the jeep.

'The north,' he supplied briefly.

'Isn't that where our hotel is?'

He gave a short laugh as they drove away. 'Yes, it is. Which is why I stay at the Sable Royale, because I can moor my boat in the lagoon, and easily get across to the island. And you don't give up, do you? Have no worries about your career, Gabriella. You'll go far.'

'Then we can take a look at it? Don't you need to see how your house is progressing?'

'We'll see. It depends on the time. And the weather.'

'But look at the sky,' she argued, gesturing towards the high, white-dotted arc of sapphire above. 'Not even a teensy little cyclone in sight!'

'Take a look behind you,' he suggested flatly. She twisted, saw the faint inky blue darkness heralding storm clouds in the distance.

'It's moving the other way,' she judged confidently.

'And you are a pushy young lady.'

It was mid-afternoon when they got back to the hotel and parked the jeep. Rick took a long, hard look at the sky and back at Gabriella's persuasive expression.

'We can go across?' she hazarded, barely restraining her excitement. He gazed at her shining dark green eyes for a moment, then shrugged.

'OK, I surrender,' he grated with wry amusement. 'Just don't blame me if we end up camping overnight with a cyclone raging all around us.'

Something in the dark gleam in his eyes gave her the unsettling impression that he might quite enjoy the challenge. She suppressed panic, and remembered her job. Ursula Taylor had sounded very keen on a small, sparsely populated island as a setting for the project. What a coup, to present her superiors with a ready-made private island for the fashion shoot, in spite of the set-back over the weather...

Her radiant smile triggered a speculative narrowing of the cool amber gaze.

'Thank you. I'm sure it won't come to that,' she said confidently, resolutely refusing to be unnerved by his mocking expression. 'And I'm sure *First Flair* will make it worth your while...'

'I sincerely hope so.' He made no attempt to expand on his cryptic comment, but such was her euphoria that she hardly noticed.

Rick's boat turned out to be a graceful white power-launch, moored at a small nearby marina. She scarcely had time to take stock of the gleaming brass rails, the mahogany fittings, the luxurious interior, before they were speeding across the clear blue waters towards the distant reef.

It was a longer trip than she'd anticipated. But at last the pearl-white gleam of a fringe of sand was visible, backed by thickets of green, then the deep emerald of the ocean began to lighten to layers of powder blue, eau-de-Nil, translucent aquamarine. The islet appeared to have its own partial coral reef, protecting it from the muted power of the ocean.

The ocean had become noticeably rougher during the trip. A darkness to the north had begun to produce some ominous-looking grey clouds, and a stronger breeze. Then they were through the narrow opening in the reef, which

Gabriella decided looked as difficult to negotiate as threading a needle blindfold, and they were slowing alongside a new-looking wooden jetty. Even in the relatively protected lagoon, the water was swelling and heaving. The trees on the island were swaying dizzily, the wind susurrating through the pine needles with a ghostly hiss.

'*Et voilà.*' Rick cut the engines, jumped out to secure the launch, and stood gazing down at her as she hesitated in the boat. There was an unfathomable expression in his eyes as he scanned the gathering clouds around them, and then studied her face. 'It looks as if we've just beaten the cyclone, Gabriella. So welcome to L'Ile des Couleuvres.'

'Ile des Coul... what?' She accepted his hand as he reached to help her out of the launch, laughing slightly to hide her flurry of reaction to his touch, as well as her secretly mounting apprehension about the weather. 'What does that mean?'

'The *couleuvre* is a small Indian snake.' He grinned as her expression switched from curiosity to alarm, tightening his grip on her hand as she made to draw back to the boat.

'Well, thanks a lot!' she managed to gasp, looking warily around her feet. 'You might have warned me I was coming to a snakes' nest!'

'It's hardly that,' he assured her calmly, leading the way from the jetty to the beach. 'Don't worry, the *couleuvre* is mainly nocturnal, and is not poisonous. I've only ever seen a couple of them, in all the times I've been here. I suspect the name was the brainwave of a long-dead Josephs to keep the island free from intruders.'

'Really?' She heard the acid note in her voice, and knew she was being deliberately awkward. She didn't really mind a few harmless little Indian snakes. 'So the island belonged to your pirate ancestors? How long have your family owned this place?'

'Since the eighteenth century.'

She was following him up the softly sloping white beach, towards the belt of *filaos*, the casuarinas which seemed to grow in profusion everywhere in this region. Dotted among them were tall coconut palms, and unknown varieties of flowering trees of such startling brightness that they looked artificial. Scarlet, yellow, deep cerise pink. Her hunch had been right; this was an absolute gem of a setting for the shoot...

'I suspect my unscrupulous ancestors used it as a useful hideaway for their buccaneering and wrecking exploits.' Rick grinned at her over his shoulder. 'There are quite a few interesting wrecks just beyond the coral reef, just as there are around most of Mauritius itself. I do a bit of diving down there, but so far no caskets of gold have emerged to prove the crimes of three hundred years ago...'

'You mean your ancestors used to deliberately *wreck* ships here?' she demanded, horrified.

The amber gaze held a teasing gleam. 'Quite likely. They were a thoroughly amoral bunch, from what I can gather. But life was hard, remember. It was every man for himself...'

'And an "imported wife" for every man?' she echoed distastefully.

'I've a feeling there was a bit of a shortage of women, despite the imports,' he mused laconically, glancing up as the sun was blotted out by a ragged black cloud. 'So they'd have two or three partners each.'

'Yes, I think I'm getting the picture! So what did your pirate ancestors do for accommodation while they were holed up here?'

'For a long time there's been a little *campement* here...'

'What's that?'

'A traditional Mauritian holiday cottage,' he grinned. 'A stone-built, thatch-roofed dwelling. That's what I'm planning on having extended and enlarged to make a full-sized house.'

'I'm surprised you'd want to build a house here and associate yourself with such a lawless history,' she said coolly, 'and as for the *snakes*...'

He stopped in mid-stride, facing her in the shadow of the *filaos*. Some of the teasing had darkened to exasperation as he caught hold of her shoulders.

'Just a minute,' he said softly, searching her face beneath the brim of her white cotton hat

with grim displeasure. 'An hour ago you were
practically begging me, come cyclone or hur-
ricane, to bring you out here, Gabriella. The least
you can do is spare me your shrewish comments!
It is impossible to believe you're only twenty-one,
when you insist on behaving like a maiden aunt
of sixty!'

'I do *not* . . . !' In the recess of her mind, she
had the sinking feeling that he was right, and that
made her feel even, angrier. 'I'm entitled to express an opinion, without being *manhandled* by
you!'

He smiled thinly, sliding his hands down her
arms and then releasing her abruptly.

'You certainly are,' he agreed evenly, his eyes
glittering with mockery. 'But if you want my co-
operation on this precious fashion shoot of yours,
mademoiselle, I strongly recommend you curb
that sharp tongue and follow a diplomatic course
from now on . . .'

The wind had risen to a low, eerie moan, and
the susurration in the trees had subtly increased
to a wilder swishing sound. She was opening her
mouth to retort when a sudden roar of wind came
rushing across the beach, whirling up a miniature
sand-storm like an invisible express train.

Terrified and bewildered, she caught the
powerful gust full in the face, and lost her
balance. Rick caught her in his arms, and she

found herself held there in surprising warmth and safety against the hardness of his chest, while the first tennis-ball-sized raindrops began pelting from a darkening sky.

CHAPTER THREE

'*MERDE*,' Rick cursed succinctly, turning to hurry her up through the trees towards the distant glimpse of a house.

'Is this the cyclone?' she gasped, breathless, as she ran along beside him.

'Full marks for observation, Gabriella.' His deep voice was grimly amused. 'Let's get under cover before we begin apportioning blame and volleying insults, shall we?'

'I wasn't going to——' The wind whipped the words from her mouth, and she gritted her teeth. The last few metres towards the *campement* felt like running up a sheer mountain weighed down with boulders, such was the effort involved in gaining momentum against the wind. Her hat had whirled skywards and disappeared, her sunglasses had fallen off and been abandoned back on the beach, and she was soaked to the skin by the time they gained the shelter of the little dwelling.

'I warn you, it's basic accommodation,' he taunted lightly, as they finally made it inside, gasping, dripping, wind-tousled.

When she'd got her breath back, she forced herself to meet his eyes, battling very hard with her temper.

'Hopefully it won't have to provide accommodation for long,' she retorted, gazing round at a flagstoned floor, masses of exposed beams, and a few pieces of rattan furniture. 'But at least it isn't a mud hut.'

'No, Miss High and Mighty Howard, not quite a mud hut...'

With an exaggerated gesture, he pulled out one of the rattan chairs, dusted it with his hand, and ushered her to sit down. Following suit beside her, he regarded her levelly, taking in the dripping hair, the white sundress plastered to her body, the wetness of her arms and legs. Suddenly acutely self-conscious, she gazed back.

'What do we do now?' she ventured at last. Outside, the storm was worsening, with a mounting roar like a jumbo jet coming in to land. Abruptly, she admitted to herself that it was the most frightening sound she'd ever heard. Her stomach in knots, she stared wide-eyed at Rick, who had an air of someone thinking fast.

'I'd say we're here for the night,' he grinned, wiping a hand over his soaked dark hair, and leaning back in his chair. 'There was every chance it would pass by without too much damage. But this sounds as if it will get a lot worse before it gets better. That being the case, I'll go back down to the boat now, and get a few provisions...'

She jumped up, startled, as he prepared to go out. 'You can't go back out there!' she cried, horrified.

'Why not? I just came in from out there, Gabriella,' he pointed out patiently. 'And now that you're safely under cover, it won't take me as long to get back to the boat. Don't worry, I'll be back soon.'

'Rick...!' She caught hold of his arm, anxiety wiping out inhibitions, making her blurt involuntarily, 'Don't leave me here on my own, please...!'

The gleam in the golden eyes intensified, but his voice was a fraction gentler when he said, 'It'll be all right, Gabriella. Just sit here, don't go anywhere, and I'll be back soon. *D'accord*?'

'But...' She swallowed hard, and nodded slowly. Her heart was thudding. With all the talk of possible cyclones, the casual reference to high winds and torrential rains, she'd never realised how terrifying a severe tropical storm could be. 'I suppose this is all my fault? I mean, if I hadn't begged you to bring me over here——'

'I take full responsibility,' he cut in calmly. 'It was my decision to come, so stop panicking. Wait for me here.' He opened the door, and the wind howled like an invisible monster through the gap. He shot her a teasing grin. 'What's that famous line from Captain Oates? "I'm going out now, and I may be some time"?'

In spite of everything, she managed a wavery smile.

'If that's supposed to be reassuring,' she protested faintly, 'Oates never came back, and the rest of Scott's expedition died!'

'But I'll be back within fifteen minutes, I promise,' he told her with quiet certainty, before the door closed decisively after him.

Alone, she drew a deep breath, ashamed of her outburst. They said a crisis brought out your true nature, didn't they? Was she such a coward, then?

And was she, heaven help her, shrewish and prudish? Did she really behave like a maiden aunt of sixty?

She gnawed her lip miserably, filled with uncertainty. Maybe, since Piers, she'd tended to be a bit prickly and frigid with men... in fact, she knew she had. It was just so hard to believe in herself, since it had all blown up in her face. So hard to believe that any man could operate without ulterior motives...

But she had been pretty tight-lipped and sarcastic, hadn't she? Rick Josephs had gone to some trouble today, put himself out, to help her. He must think she was the most ungrateful, ill-tempered female he'd ever met. And the feeblest...

Since it was more than partly her fault that they were in this mess, the least she could do was abandon self-pity, try being positive...

She got up, forced herself into action. Was there any food here? Electricity? Checking in cupboards in the tiny kitchen, she dubiously eyed the remains of some charcoal and a makeshift barbecue. But yes, there seemed to be electricity. There were also some candles in a drawer, and a Calor gas cooker.

Things could be a great deal worse, she told herself firmly, beginning an inspection of the small cottage. They could have been stranded here with no shelter at all. They could have been caught in this storm in the middle of the Indian Ocean, being tossed around helplessly on thirty-foot waves at this very moment...

The cottage was all on one floor, flagstoned throughout. It had a large sitting-room, with a terrace overlooking the sea. When there wasn't a cyclone howling outside, she imagined this would be a very pleasant place to sit in the evening, shaded by an extension of the thatched roof. There was a bathroom, and a loo. Air-conditioning throughout consisted of the traditional variety, electric ceiling fans. When Rick said 'basic', she assumed he was judging it by the standards he was used to wherever he normally lived, be it New York, Paris or London. Because in a rustic way it had a certain charm. White walls bore paintings, their colourful style possibly that of a local artist. There was even a bookcase full of books, an eclectic selection in French and English, featuring a lot of travel, photography, and medieval detective stories. What furniture there was consisted of pine or rattan, giving a fresh country feel.

Walking into the bedroom, she stopped in her tracks.

There was one small square bedroom, and only one bed, a double bed, an old pine one which looked far from luxurious, bereft of sheets or blankets.

Her heart plummeted again. She went hot, then cold. There was no way on earth she was spending the night with Rick Josephs in a double bed. She'd rather sleep on the floor——

'I see you've found the sleeping quarters,' he said behind her, making her jump convulsively. Swinging round, she saw that he was soaked to the skin, and carried two enormous waterproof holdalls, bulging at the sides with their contents.

'I didn't hear you come back in,' she said breathlessly, pressing her hand to her heart to control the wildly erratic thudding. 'You startled me...'

He dropped the holdalls on the floor, and frowned at her pallor with a gleam of concern. 'Calm down, Gabriella. You're jumpy as a cat.'

'Yes. I know. It's this wind. It sounds as if the world's coming to an end any moment...'

He grinned, raking his fingers through his dripping hair and nodding wryly. 'My guess is that the world will manage to spin on for a while longer after this cyclone has blown itself out,' he reassured her, bending to unzip the holdalls. In some amazement, she realised that he had sleeping-bags, towels, some rolled-up shorts and T-shirts, plus bottled water and a coolbag of food.

'I could suspect you of planning this in advance,' she pointed out, half jokingly.

'With a suspicious little mind like yours, Gabriella, that doesn't surprise me.' He straightened up, tossing the sleeping-bags on to the bed, and dropping the towels over the back of a chair. 'Just for the record, the launch is always kitted out for overnight trips. When I'm coming out to Mauritius, an agency stocks the fridge for me.'

'Yes. I believe you,' she added with a touch of impatience, hesitating as she glanced back at the bed. 'I'm not terribly happy about... about sharing the bed!'

'Is that a fact?' His expression was far from sympathetic as he took the food and water back to the kitchen. 'Well, you're welcome to a sleeping-bag on the floor, with the odd stray *couleuvre* for company, *ma petite*,' he called back over his shoulder. 'I regret I am not quite so chivalrous.'

'I see . . .' She was hot all over as he turned that mocking gaze on her. The heat once again turned to shivers, and with a convulsive shudder she wrapped her arms around herself, and sat down abruptly on one of the rattan chairs.

Rick surveyed her for a long, thoughtful moment, then dumped the food on the small pine table in the kitchen and came back to haul her to her feet.

'Go into the bedroom, and put some dry clothes on,' he advised firmly. 'There is a towel, and some shorts and T-shirts. They may not be *haute couture*, but you should get out of those wet things.'

'Yes. You're right.' She turned to go, then paused, determinedly making an effort. 'When I come back, I'll see if I can "play house", shall I? Rustle up some wonderful meal from whatever you've got in that coolbag?'

He shrugged, smiling slightly. His eyes took in her slender figure in the wet white dress, the strands of dishevelled blonde hair escaping the plait, her goose-bump-covered arms and legs. His gaze softened a fraction.

'Whatever keeps you happy, Gabriella,' he agreed calmly. 'It could be a long night.'

The clothes Rick had brought from the boat were obviously his. They were enormous on Gabriella. Emerging after some vigorous towelling, clad in tightly belted khaki shorts, rolled up at the legs, and an oversize black T-shirt, she felt marginally better. The shivers remained, but at least she felt dry, and warmer.

'I'll go and do the same,' Rick said, casting an amused glance over her appearance. 'I've boiled some water for coffee.'

'Right...' She kept her voice as brisk as she could. This enforced domesticity felt unnervingly normal, as if she'd spent the night with him in an isolated *campement* during a raging cyclone dozens of times before.

Taking over the coffee-making, she found long-life milk, then realised she didn't even know how Rick took his coffee. Black or white, sugar or no sugar. She knew absolutely nothing about him, she acknowledged with a jolt. And here she was, alone with him, marooned for the moment on an uninhabited island, calmly making coffee...

'That smells good. No milk, thanks. Or sugar.'

He'd towel-dried his hair, and it fell in a tousled dark lock over his forehead. In white Bermudas, and a loose navy sweatshirt, he looked fresh and relaxed, as if he hadn't a care in the world.

'I took a shower. Go ahead if you want one.'

'Oh, yes. I didn't think of that. Will anyone be worrying about us?' she wondered suddenly, sitting down with her own milky coffee.

'I radioed back to the marina from the boat,' he explained briefly. 'They'll let the hotel know. And they'll either expect us back when the storm has died down, or send my Jet Ranger over to pick us up.'

'Oh...' She sipped the coffee, glancing at her watch, and frowning out of the window. 'It'll be dark any minute now, won't it? Thank goodness this place has got electricity.'

'That could go down at any moment, the way the storm is escalating,' he told her, with a bleak smile. 'So if you want a hot shower, now's the time to take one.'

'You mean we could be blacked out totally?'

'We have candles. There's some wood beside the fireplace—I could light a fire if it will cheer you up?'

'That might be nice...' She shivered again, and rubbed her fingers over her forehead. She felt odd, not ill exactly, but slightly light-headed. 'Actually, would you mind if I did have a hot shower?'

'Go ahead, Gabriella,' he grinned. 'And if you keep up this civil behaviour until we get out of here, I'll take back all my criticisms.'

She decided this didn't merit a reply.

The tropical darkness fell abruptly, speeded up by the storm-blackened sky. The light glowed cosily in the simple, whitewashed bathroom as she stepped into the shower, and revelled in the warmth and comfort of the jets of hot water. She was beginning to feel marginally recovered from her attack of shivers and dizziness, when everything went black, and the shower ran cold.

Letting out a muffled shriek, she fumbled desperately for the tap, stumbled out of the cubicle, feeling in pitch-darkness for the towel. Without light, the sound of the cyclone shrieking around the house seemed a hundred times more alarming.

'Are you all right, Gabriella?' Rick's voice, cool and controlled, called from outside the door.

'Yes...no...oh, *damn*...' She stubbed her toe on the side of the bath, and doubled up in pain, dripping wet and beginning to shiver more violently. 'I can't find the *towel*...'

'Don't panic, I'm bringing you a candle,' he stated flatly, opening the door. The glow from the candle in his hand filled the small room, and Gabriella dropped her fingers from rubbing her toes and searched wildly for the elusive towel.

Bending down, Rick retrieved it from where it had slipped off the side of the bath on to the floor. He held it out to her, his expression deadpan. Grabbing it, she swathed herself with shaking fingers, conscious of Rick's steady gaze on her naked body in the candlelight.

'Seen enough?' she demanded furiously. She was close to tears, she realised, her pride badly wounded.

'Enough to wonder why you're so defensive about such a beautiful body,' he murmured calmly, depositing the candles on a shelf and turning to go. There was an unreadable gleam in his eyes as he glanced back over his shoulder, adding, 'I've lit the fire. I'm making my own sketchy interpretation of the local cuisine. Come when you're ready.'

Already ashamed of the violence of her re-action to the incident, she clutched the towel round herself and nodded wordlessly.

The fire was licking into healthy life when she finally plucked up courage to join him. An extraordinarily appetising smell was wafting from the small kitchen. Everywhere flickered with candlelight, giving a deceptively festive appearance.

'What on earth are you cooking?' she enquired, forcing a bright smile as she came to peer over his shoulder. On the small Calor stove some rice was simmering in a pan, and in a wok sizzled what looked like strips of bacon, chicken, and various unidentifiable vegetables.

'Whatever I found in the boat fridge, plus a bottle of curry sauce,' he told her, eyeing her enquiringly. 'Recovered from your ordeal just now?'

'Yes. I'm sorry I... reacted the way I did...'

'You don't need to apologise,' he assured her drily, the golden gaze darkening a fraction as he raked her up and down. 'At the sight of you wearing nothing but a glare, my thoughts were far from pure, I'll admit.'

She found herself blushing to the roots of her hair at the kindling flicker in his eyes.

'So you're quite right to keep up the defences, Gabriella,' he mocked softly, stirring the miscellaneous contents of the wok with a practised flick of a wooden spatula. 'Who knows what wickedly depraved males may claim as their right, if you don't?'

'Quite,' she agreed flippantly, glancing round for something to do. 'Shall I drain the rice?'

'Sure. You can take over here, if you like. I'll open some wine. Red or white? Or can I tempt you to some chilled champagne?'

She avoided the provocation. 'Red, please.'

She felt in need of something vaguely medicinal. Her head throbbed, her throat felt slightly sore. Red wine sounded more soothing than white . . .

'This is intimate,' he taunted a short while later, as they ate the concocted supper in the fire and candlelight. 'Nothing like a cyclone for forcing people to eat dinner together.'

'Whatever this mixture is,' she informed him, with a half-smile, 'it's an inspired creation. Now I know what your secret occupation is: you're a famous chef.'

'Flattery?' he queried drily. 'You're making me nervous, Gabriella. Surely my occupation is no secret? World-class playboy and philanderer, isn't it?'

'I imagine there's a little more to it than that,' she countered uncertainly, taking a long drink of wine, and laying down her fork. The noise of the storm had risen from jumbo jet to a full-scale invasion of fighter planes. They had to raise their voices to make themselves heard. 'It's funny, but if I were stranded here alone, with that violent storm howling outside, I'd be absolutely terrified. So I'm grateful to you for making me feel less terrified.'

'Any time,' he grinned, inspecting the ruby gleam of wine in his glass, then directing a disconcertingly level gaze at her across the table. 'Tell me, what has happened in your life to make you so defensive, Gabriella? A bad childhood? A love-affair?'

'My childhood was very happy, thanks,' she informed him, suddenly wary again.

'Then an unhappy love-affair it has to be,' Rick mused speculatively. 'What happened? Would it help to tell me about it?'

Tell Rick Josephs the humiliating story of her ordeal with Piers? She'd rather die!

'No, frankly, it wouldn't,' she informed him flatly, softening the rebuttal with a cool smile. 'You're not exactly the kind of man to invite confidences, you know. I've never met anyone as cagey as you are!'

'You seem quite happy drawing your own conclusions.'

She stared at him, feeling a familiar stab of frustration. 'Meaning?'

'Meaning that you appear to have preconceived notions of what goes on in other people's lives, Gabriella.'

'You mean about my jumping to the conclusion that you're having an affair with Ursula Taylor?' She felt her face go pinker. 'I . . . apologise. I had no right to jump to such a conclusion. But . . . are you?' she queried simply.

He was silent for a long moment, his gaze darkening ominously. 'I can see no reason why I should confirm or deny it to you,' he murmured finally, his voice cool. 'But nor do I see any reason why you should have reached that conclusion, on the evidence to date.'

'Maybe we're delving into rather muddy waters,' she said shortly. He really was highly skilled at evasive replies. She thought about the beautiful girls at the bar, and decided not to pursue that subject either. Switching to safer ground, she said casually, 'Why on earth do you stay at the Sable Royale, when you've got this place over here?'

His eyes gleamed with amusement. 'You like it?'

'Yes, I think it's lovely...'

'I don't recall saying I never stay here,' he informed her quietly. 'I often come here for a night or two. But if I have any business to attend to, it's more convenient to be at a hotel on Mauritius.'

'Oh, I see...' The shivers were back. Plus a few new aches and pains. Pushing her plate away, she finished her wine, and then rose shakily to her feet. 'I'm sorry, I'm afraid I'm not feeling quite right...'

'Apologising again?' he teased, coming round the table to take hold of her arm. 'This is getting to be a habit. You're looking very flushed and bright-eyed, Gabriella. Do you feel feverish?'

'I'm not sure how I feel...what was *that* noise?' She flinched as a crashing sound penetrated above the steady roar of the wind outside. Rick slid his arm tightly around her shoulders, drawing her closer.

'A tree uprooting, I'd say. Come on, you could do with going to bed.'

'I...yes, I think you're right,' she admitted miserably, suddenly too light-headed to object to being lifted easily into his arms, and carried through to the bedroom. Laying her on the bed, he went to fetch a candle, returning to touch his palm to her forehead, frowning down at her.

'You're burning up,' he said, his voice level but his eyes preoccupied. 'Not the most convenient moment to run a temperature, Gabriella.'

He was joking, she knew, but suddenly she felt tears sting her eyes. Ashamed of herself, she found her voice choked with frustrated emotion as she said, 'What do you think's wrong with me?'

'Well, at a rough guess,' he said, sitting down beside her, and taking her hand between both of his in a gentle, almost brotherly way, 'you've gone down with *First Flair* fashion department's notorious flu!'

'Oh, *no*...!' Rolling against the pillow, she closed her eyes in despair.

'However, Dr Josephs to the rescue,' he went on thoughtfully, 'because I may have some aspirin in the boat...'

'In the boat?' Panic made her lever herself up, and she clutched at his hand. 'Rick, you are *not* to go out again. Do you hear me? I'd rather die, right here, tonight, than let you go out in that wind again! Promise me!'

'Hey, calm down...' He was looking at her with bemused humour. 'I concede it may be a bit of a risk, but I'm quite happy to oblige for a lady...'

'No, *no*! Promise me you'll stay here with me?' she cried unsteadily. 'Please?'

'OK. Anything you say. I'll stay here with you,' he grinned, a wicked gleam in his eyes as he spread out one of the sleeping-bags, and helped her into it. 'You're probably right, it would have been gallantry on a potentially life-threatening level...' The grin grew wider as suspicion tinged her eyes. 'But it is nice to know you care so much for my safety, Gabriella!'

'You...*fraud*!' she managed to gasp, her sense of humour fighting through. 'How can you still tease me, when I'm feeling so awful...?'

'At least I've made you laugh,' he pointed out, zipping up the side of the sleeping-bag, and observing the conflicting emotions on her face with an enigmatic gaze. 'Now think hard; do you have something with you to take, to bring down the fever? Pain-killers in your bag, perhaps?'

She shook her head, wincing as a shaft of pain stabbed her forehead. 'Nothing...back at the hotel, in my luggage, but not with me today...'

She groaned, giving in to a sudden wave of acute self-pity and guilt. 'Oh, hell, I feel such an idiot... What on earth am I going to *do*?'

'You'll just have to sweat it out in the old-fashioned way,' he told her, with grim sympathy. 'And from the feel of your body heat, *ma petite*, we could be in for a rough night, in more ways than one!'

CHAPTER FOUR

THE suddenness with which the fever soared was almost as unnerving as the onslaught of the cyclone. One minute Gabriella was lying there with a thudding headache, and an ache in every limb, the next she was shivering so violently that her teeth were chattering.

Coming back into the bedroom with a glass of water, Rick frowned at her hectic cheeks and over-bright eyes. He bent to smooth a hand over her damp forehead, and muttered something unrepeatable under his breath. Gabriella stared up at him, hazily conscious of his nearness, of the alarming way her pulses seemed to quicken at his touch. How could this insidious attraction still overwhelm her, when she was probably dying of pneumonia or something?

'Come on, you'd better get out of those clothes,' he suggested wryly, unzipping the sleeping-bag again. 'You can't sweat out a fever fully dressed.'

'I can manage by myself,' she protested weakly. Through the throb of her headache, she blinked at him indignantly in the flickering candlelight.

'OK, prove it,' he teased, drily amused. But her limbs felt abnormally heavy, as if she was working against some invisible force simply to lift a hand off the bed. Her head, too, felt three times its normal weight. If only this uncontrollable shivering would let up for a moment. Her face was beginning to ache with the involuntary spasm of her jaw. Striving to lever herself up off the bed felt like climbing through thick, dark treacle. She would achieve the movement required, she felt sure, but only in exceptionally slow motion.

He watched her struggle for a few seconds, then scooped one strong arm round her and pulled her to a sitting position, firmly beginning to seek the fastening of the shorts.

Between chattering teeth, she said, 'I can *manage* . . . ! Are you deaf or something?'

'Or something,' he agreed, infuriatingly bland. Long brown fingers expertly flicked open the waistband, slid down the zip, and she found herself pushed down against the pillow as he eased the shorts over her narrow hips, taking her brief white silk panties along with them. Rigid with shocked embarrassment, she writhed beneath his hands. The masked quality of his expression did nothing for her morale. If he was going to ravish her, the least he could do was look *interested*, she thought irrationally. . .

'No bra?' With a methodical coolness, he scanned the firm swell of her breasts beneath the thin fabric, slipping his hands beneath the over-sized black T-shirt, and checking for straps against the silky heat of her back.

Mortified, burning with more than fever, she remained motionless, feeling like a lifeless mannequin in a shop window display. But closing her eyes, despite the aches and shivers of her fever, there were a million tiny erotic messages scurrying between the surface of her skin and her nerve-centres...

'All right, Gabriella, you can relax. I told you before, you're safe—I'm no cradle-snatcher, *ma petite.*'

'*Cradle-snatcher*?' she heard herself protest thickly. 'I'm not a child; I told you, I'm twenty-one! How old are you?'

'Thirty-four,' he supplied shortly, 'but I'm mature for my age, whereas you're definitely immature for yours, Gabriella.'

'So modest!' she managed through her shivers. 'And if I'm so *safe*, how come you were thinking those impure thoughts when you saw me in the bathroom?'

'I don't recall saying that I find you...sexually unattractive,' he replied evenly, sitting down on the bed, and half covering her with the sleeping-bag again. 'I'm just saying that I've no intention of doing anything about it. My life's complicated enough right now, without seducing flu-stricken adolescents. Have you got a sore throat?'

'N-no, just the headache to end all headaches, and I can't stop shivering. And don't call me adolescent! I stopped being one at the age of about nineteen...'

'Decades ago, in fact,' he mocked softly. 'And yours is a case of arrested development.'

'Oh, lord...' she moaned into her pillow, half crying, half laughing. 'I must have done something really terrible to be punished like this—marooned on an island with flu and *you* as my night nurse!'

'I'm not ecstatic about the situation either.'

'No. Well, I'm sorry to be such a pain...'

'Don't start apologising again,' he said abruptly. 'Just try a little co-operation, *d'accord*?'

Duly chastened, she blinked at him, her eyes dark green pools in the pallor of her face.

'Point taken,' she murmured blearily. The shivering had stopped, replaced by a burning heat which threatened to melt her bones. After the shivering it was almost a relief, if it weren't for the persistent aching of her limbs, and her spine, and her head. The effort of speaking was growing too much. 'From now on, co-operation will be my... middle name...'

Sleepiness was engulfing her. Outside, the cyclone shrieked and moaned like a thousand souls in torment. In the sanctuary of the bedroom, the candlelight flickered and wavered. It threw shadows across the ceiling, and cast Rick's face into dark relief. She fell into a hot, fitful sleep, her subconscious imprinted with the vivid image of him as he sat with her.

Expressionless as a sphinx, his jaw darkened by the dusky shading of five-o'clock stubble, he looked tough, remote, as if he were a complete stranger...

Her dreams were full of storms, snakes and pirates. She was trapped, taken hostage, surrounded by danger and darkness. A wild wind blew, and fierce men with knives and cutlasses abounded. Someone had pinned her to the deck of a ship, bound her tightly so that she couldn't escape. Despite the storm, somehow the midday sun baked down from an unremitting blue sky, heating her skin, hotter and hotter, until she was catching fire, burning with no escape...she called out for help, and the man who came wore a mask, a black mask. She thought it was Rick, but when he bent over her and lifted the mask he was Piers, dark blond hair flopping forwards over languid, lidded grey eyes. He held a cutlass in his hand, raised above her, his intention not to cut her loose but to commit some act of violence, and with all her remaining strength she fought like a wildcat to save herself...

'Gabriella...Gabriella...hey, it's all right, it's all right...' The deep, gravelly voice finally penetrated the layers of fever and nightmare. Cool hands were disentangling her from the damp covering of her sleeping-bag. She opened her eyes to find herself in Rick's arms, hot and shivering, the black T-shirt clammy around her.

'What? What's happening...?' Completely disorientated, she struggled for a few moments, then subsided limply against his chest.

'Briefly, you're trying to beat me to death in my sleep,' he supplied huskily. 'I'm tempted to try out the floor for the rest of the night!'

Moving her gently off him, he leaned to light another candle, then inspected her with a grim glint in his eyes.

'You're soaked,' he pointed out unnecessarily, lifting the hem of the sweat-damp T-shirt. 'I'll get you another T-shirt.'

Too weak to protest, she submitted to the replacement of the black T-shirt with a dry bottle-green one, equally capacious.

'I think I've cracked the mystery of your profession,' she murmured faintly, as she hugged the fresh one around herself and avoided his eyes. 'You're a T-shirt manufacturer?'

He grinned suddenly, his teeth white in his dark face. 'Wrong again. I'll get you some more water...' His voice was wry as he went off to the kitchen, returning with a glass. 'How do you feel now?'

'Awful,' she said hoarsely, sipping the water. 'As if I've argued with a juggernaut. I ache all over. I was having the most horrible dream— snakes, pirates, men with knives, and...'

'Piers?' he queried innocently. Gabriella focused on him from beneath heavy lids, temporarily thrown. Then the truth dawned—she'd said the name in her sleep?

Putting down the glass with a clatter on the bedside table, she collapsed back against the pillow, and closed her eyes.

'Yes, Piers was in it...' she mumbled miserably, waves of nausea creeping over her as the shivers began again. 'Oh, lord, I think I'm dying...'

'Healthy twenty-one-year-olds don't die from a touch of flu,' Rick informed her bluntly. 'Even if they are deprived of aspirin.'

But his hand was gentle as he stroked her hot forehead. Tendrils of blonde hair had escaped her plait, curling slightly from their soaking in the rain. He pushed them from her eyes. His touch was confident, inspiring confidence. Half aware, half drifting again into the fluctuating bouts of near-delirium, she was conscious nevertheless of liking the sensation to an alarming degree...

The bed dipped as he left her again, and she felt bereft. The roar of the storm outside was still as disturbingly violent. When she surfaced blearily from her half-doze, the bedroom with its flickering candle seemed surreal, frightening. When the bed dipped again, and she knew he'd returned, the relief was intense. He pressed something cool and damp over her forehead, and, hardly knowing what she was doing, she clung to him, moving as close as she could and wrapping her arms round him.

'Don't go again,' she managed faintly. 'Don't leave me alone...'

The last thing she recalled before falling into another feverish, delirious sleep was Rick's arms tightening around her, drawing her down against his chest, his hand stroking her hair in a soothing, rhythmical motion which made her feel safe, and protected, and ridiculously, irrationally happy...

The next time she woke, it was daylight. Not sunny, but a bright light filtering through bamboo blinds. For the first few moments she grappled mentally to work out where she was. Physically drained, she stared blankly at white walls, a rattan-framed mirror, a stripped-pine door. Then she struggled to sit up, and memory returned with a jolt. Rick's island. The cyclone. Flu...

She was alone in bed. Blinking, cautiously widening her eyes, she hauled herself into a sitting position, all her senses alert, unsure what seemed so different. Then she realised. The wind had stopped. Instead of a noise in the air like a tube train coming into an underground station, there was only the gentlest rustle of breeze in the trees outside the open window. The cyclone was over.

Warily twisting round on the bed, she lowered her legs tentatively to the floor, and tested her weight. Someone seemed to have extracted every last ounce of strength from her leg muscles. The bathroom wasn't very far away, but her progress towards it resembled moon-walking, slow-motion. She was at the bedroom door, her hand on the knob, when it opened, throwing her off-balance. Swaying precariously, Rick stepped inside and caught her firmly by the arms.

She stared at him. He'd found a razor, evidently, because he looked clean-shaven. In white Bermudas and a navy T-shirt, he was tall, muscular, infinitely disturbing to her beleaguered senses...

'Good morning.' His expression was unreadable as he looked her over. 'You've surfaced at last. Bravo.'

'What time is it?'

'It might be more interesting to ask what day it is,' he teased lightly, slipping a hand round her back and propelling her to the bathroom door. 'I assume you're heading this way? If you want a shower, the electricity's back on, so it can't have been the worst cyclone in our history——'

'What do you mean,' she interrupted, 'about asking what day it is? It's Wednesday, isn't it? The day after yesterday...?'

'Wrong. Thursday. You've missed a day completely.'

'I've what?' She stopped dead, gazed at him in horror, clutching the door-frame for support. 'Are you serious?'

'Totally.'

'I've missed a day...doing what? Sleeping?'

'Mainly sleeping. In between feverish rambling and making erotic suggestions to me...'

She flushed deeply, glaring at his mocking amber eyes. 'I didn't...!'

'Don't panic, I didn't take you up on any of them.'

If only she had the strength to slap his sardonic face!

'I can't have done! And even if I did, it's extremely ungentlemanly of you to tell me! Oh, lord, what about my *job*? They'll all have arrived in Mauritius by now, won't they? And I've done nothing...!'

'Calm down, Gabriella,' he advised. 'Even if you hadn't had the flu, there was nothing you could do until the cyclone was over. And what about all those notes you made on our tour of Mauritius? All the photographs you took? You can't say you've done nothing, when you've worked very hard.'

'Yes, but I must get back now...'

'Hurry up in the bathroom, and then go back to bed,' he ordered flatly. 'You're not going anywhere.'

'Now just a minute...'

'Do as you're told.' Rick's voice held a steely note. There was a warning glint in the amber eyes. 'Nobody runs a temperature like you did and goes dashing back to work the next day, Gabriella.'

'I think I could be the judge of that...' she began stiffly, then stopped, abruptly conscious of the state she must be in, of how she must look. Rumpled, unwashed, thoroughly unappetising.

Swinging away from him, her head reeling unpleasantly from the abrupt motion, she went inside the bathroom and slammed the door, locking it behind her.

'Leave it unlocked,' he advised shortly. 'I don't want to waste energy kicking it down if you pass out in there.'

Rigid with indignation, she glared at the bolt for a few seconds, and then shot it back and called shakily, 'OK, but don't you dare come barging in!'

'Don't concern yourself.' His voice was growing more distant as he walked away. 'I've already seen it all, remember?'

Remember? How could she forget? As she switched on the shower, she flinched with humiliation. How *could* the wretched man tease her about anything she might have said or done in her delirious state? But her indignation began to fade as the sheer effort of washing herself began to drain her energy. She found some shampoo, and forced herself to wash her hair. She soaped herself all over with some sandalwood-scented soap. Then she availed herself of some spearmint toothpaste from the ledge over the basin, and used her finger to brush her teeth.

Feeling a fraction more human, but utterly exhausted, she managed to get her T-shirt back on, a white one with a batik print of palm leaves. How many T-shirts had she got through in the last twenty-four hours? How many occasions had

Rick exchanged a sweat-soaked one for a dry one?

The knowledge that Rick Josephs had repeatedly dressed and undressed her like a sick child sent a fresh shiver of mortification through her. Setting her teeth, she wrapped her wet hair in a dark blue towel, and staggered on rubber legs back to the bedroom.

Rick was there, reclining in one of the rattan chairs. Coffee in a beautiful old silver pot, and a dish of warm rolls awaited her, on a low, glass-topped table.

'Can you manage some breakfast?' he smiled, as she sank on to the bed.

'Yes, I suppose so...' She pulled the towel from her hair, and made a half-hearted attempt to rub it dry. It fell in a thick, damp tangle over her shoulders.

'You could sound more grateful,' he reprimanded teasingly. 'I've been working very hard while you've been comatose.'

He laid a wicker tray on her lap, complete with a spray of papery, delicate pink flowers in a tiny silver vase. Taking the wet blue towel, he slung it over the end of the bed, and went back to drink his coffee.

'What a lovely flower!' Despite her wariness and exhaustion, she couldn't help smiling, feeling an involuntary lift of the spirits. 'What is it?'

'It's bougainvillaea. Salvaged from the remains...'

'Oh!' For the first time, it dawned on her that after the ferocious winds wide-scale destruction must have taken place outside. 'Has the storm caused a lot of damage?'

'Not too bad. The wind probably didn't exceed eighty or ninety miles an hour, gusting to a hundred at times. This old place has withstood a lot worse. A few *filaos* were flattened. Some palms were uprooted. A few more could still be unstable, so it will pay to take care when you do go out...but the cyclones in Mauritius have been a lot more dramatic. Cyclone Gervaise in 1975 had winds gusting up to 174 miles an hour.'

She shuddered, spreading butter and apricot jam from a small pot, and taking a bite of the crusty roll. She was hungry. Ravenously hungry, she discovered. Not surprising, if Rick was telling the truth about her lost day.

'You said you've been working very hard. What have you been doing?'

'You really want to know? *Eh bien*, there is good news and bad news, as the saying goes.' He gave her a rueful grin. 'Which would you like first?'

'The bad news?' She felt her stomach contract apprehensively.

'OK. The bad news is that the motor-launch was one of the casualties of the cyclone...'

'*What* ...?' In her jerk of dismay, she almost toppled the white porcelain coffee-cup and the silver vase. 'You mean we're really marooned? We can't get back ... ?'

He laughed at her aghast expression.

'The situation is not quite so melodramatic, *ma petite*. The launch is still there; it has not been blown out to sea. However, it will not get us back to Mauritius, and sadly there is no radio contact.' He paused, an amused glint in his eyes as if he saw the entire episode as some highly entertaining diversion. 'But the good news is that the stores on board are accessible. We therefore have plenty of bottled water, food, and an adequate supply of casual clothing ...'

'There can't be any T-shirts left, surely?'

'One or two,' he grinned, appreciating her irony. 'While I don't personally make T-shirts, I confess they are an article manufactured in abundance on Mauritius.'

'You've got shares in T-shirt factories!' she decided, feeling fractionally better after another sip of the delicious, aromatic coffee.

'Perhaps I have,' he agreed non-committally. 'Tell me, what sort of clothes are *First Flair* magazine planning to photograph when they finally make it over here?'

'Beach clothes, mainly. There's a new ethnic range by a young designer not long out of college—a lot of Eastern influence. Ursula thought Mauritius would make an apt setting.'

Mentioning Ursula's name brought reality flooding back, in the shape of her job, her responsibilities, the high hopes she'd had of making an efficient impression. With a groan, she put her cup down in the saucer, and raked her fingers through her damp hair.

'I really should be there,' she said anxiously. 'What on earth are they going to think if I've gone missing?'

'First, it's doubtful if they've arrived yet. Cyclones are notorious for cancelling aeroplane flights, Gabriella. Second, you can't be blamed for catching the bug which has laid the entire department low already. Third, you haven't gone missing. If you recall, I radioed when the cyclone first hit. The marina and the hotel both know where we are. When we don't return, they'll send someone over.'

She stared at him, her throat tight with a complex mixture of anger and resentment.

'How can you be so...philosophical?' she burst out. 'Don't you have any commitments? Are you so totally idle it makes no difference to be holed up on some God-forsaken island for goodness knows how long, with someone you despise?'

There was a long silence following this outburst. Gabriella, shaking from the effort, subsided against the pillow, catching her lower lip in her teeth. Finally, Rick said, ominously softly, 'With someone you despise, Gabriella? Are you suggesting that I despise you? Or is it the other way around, I wonder?'

'I . . .' She wished desperately she'd restrained her emotional attack. It wasn't as if it even made sense. Not now. Rick's fleeting likeness, in her own imagination, to Piers Wellington had long since faded into oblivion.

There was no way Piers would have coped with this situation, she reflected with a flash of illumination. The thought of having to care for someone too feverish to know night from day, of having to brave a violent tropical cyclone to get the supplies from the launch, would have had Piers running fast in the opposite direction, or moodily blaming everyone else for the tricky situation he found himself in . . .

'Rick . . .' she began, struggling to compose her thoughts.

'Tell me,' he cut in coolly, 'what exactly is it you despise me for, Gabriella? Are you in the habit of passing snap judgements on people you hardly know?'

'No, I——'

'You imagine you know my lifestyle, perhaps? You have a firm opinion of me as a philanderer? An adulterer? A marriage-wrecker? A seducer of tipsy young women at hotel bars?' The deep voice was without inflexion, as calmly polite as if he were enquiring about the weather. Heat suffused her face, and then faded again.

'I didn't mean . . .'

'So what did you mean? Come, Gabriella, I am interested to know what goes on behind that beautiful mask of yours,' he persisted tauntingly. 'You have the blonde hair and green eyes of a siren, but the soul of a frigid little manhater...'

'Stop it!' The words emerged as a husky sob. Tears filling her eyes, she stared at him in a turmoil of uncertainty. 'I'm sorry. OK? I'm sorry! I didn't mean that I despise you! I don't, I admire you, and I'm grateful for the way you've looked after me...' She swallowed on a hard lump in her throat, and went on shakily, 'If I've appeared to...to judge you, it's because you...you reminded me of someone I was very unhappy with...'

'Ah. Don't tell me. Piers?' The harsh taunt came as no surprise. She'd been expecting him to bring up Piers's name again, after her feverish rantings.

'Yes. Piers.' For the life of her, she couldn't go on. She just stared at him in dumb misery, all the humiliation and disillusion of the Piers saga swirling back to rob her of her self-confidence, prick the healing wounds into fresh stinging...

'Tell me about Piers.' It was more a command than a question. 'He's the unhappy love-affair I guessed at. Correct?'

She hesitated a moment, struggling with her pride. Then she nodded slowly.

'Yes...'

To her horror, large tears welled up under her lowered lids, and trickled blatantly down her cheeks. There was nothing she could do to suppress them; they welled and rolled with a will of their own.

With a suppressed expletive, Rick stood up and came across to the bed. He took the tray, and put it aside, then sat beside her, pulling her into his arms. He held her against his chest, and the convulsive breath she drew in reverberated through him.

'Hell! Gabriella, don't cry...' he grated remorsefully, his face against her hair as he pressed her head against him with a hard embrace. 'I've no right to lose my patience with you, when you've been ill. Don't cry. It's all right. Hush...'

'No, it's not all right,' she sobbed, hardly knowing what she said, 'Piers was such an absolute bastard! I can't think why you reminded me of him, even fleetingly. It's not even as if you're physically like him. He's blond, and you're dark. He's very slim, and you're not...well, you're not fat exactly but...'

Rick had begun to laugh again. She could feel the vibration of his rich, deep chuckle of amusement.

'I'm not fat exactly?' he echoed incredulously, the flat muscular plane of his diaphragm evident beneath her cheek, the lean tautness of his stomach and pelvic region disturbingly close to her breasts. 'With company such as yours, Gabriella, a man could suffer from an ego so inflated he might never be the same again...'

'I—I mean, you're the opposite to Piers,' she stammered, the warmth from his lean body beginning adversely to affect her immune system. 'He's sort of... languid. Elegant. You're all hard muscle and sinew and... and all...'

'All male?' he finished for her drily, his expression subtly changing as he drew her up to look into her flushed face.

There was a difference in the golden gaze. The pupils were widely dilated, darkening his eyes, and triggering an instinctive, neuro-chemical response in her own reflexes. Catching her breath disbelievingly, she felt her body melting in his embrace, her nervous system jumping wildly out of control as the message in his eyes was mirrored by her own reactions.

'So this Piers hurt you?' he questioned hoarsely. His deep voice had thickened. 'And I remind you of him? Perhaps it's time for an accurate comparison, Gabriella. Perhaps it's time to see how far I remind you of him...'

CHAPTER FIVE

FROM the way Rick kissed her, Gabriella had the feeling it was meant only to last a few seconds, a hard, questioning exploration of her lips, to imprint his identity firmly over that of the absent Piers.

Somewhere along the way, it became more than that. She wasn't certain if it was her response, or his, but abruptly the tension escalated. His lips moved to deepen the kiss, covering hers, his tongue seeking entry between her teeth to delve inside the intimate warmth of her mouth. And with a powerful surge of emotion, triggering restless shivers from the tips of her breasts to her groin, she opened her mouth wide, blind to all else, and ardently, fiercely, she kissed him back...

With a muffled groan against her lips, Rick drew back a fraction, cupping her face in his hands, searching her lidded green eyes with a gaze darkening with desire.

'Gabriella...kissing you isn't enough...' It was a thick, strangled request for help, she dimly registered...he was asking her to resist...

But for some reason she found that she didn't want to resist. Because he was right. Kissing wasn't enough any more, she acknowledged hazily, using this brave realisation as a lame excuse for putting up no fight whatsoever against the lean hand skimming hungrily beneath her T-shirt, outlining the slender length of her back and the slim curve of her hips. She wore nothing beneath the T-shirt. Hearing his rough intake of breath as she pressed against him and slid warm arms around his waist, she shuddered in astonishment at her own need. Was this madness a typical after-effect of the flu? she wondered in a daze, gasping as Rick cursed softly and flattened her beside him on the bed.

'Gabriella, I shouldn't be doing this,' he whispered unevenly, the gleam in the amber eyes deepening with desire. 'But after all my high-minded promise I confess I want you very badly... I'm burning up for you! Just tell me to stop, *ma petite*, and God help me I'll try...'

'Rick... I don't...' Moving restlessly, feverish with a different kind of fever, she let her hands follow their own inclinations, stroking up the muscular ridges of his back beneath the navy T-shirt, feeling him tense even harder under her touch. 'I must be crazy, but this feels so right... Rick, I don't want you to stop...'

This was too much for his tenuous self-restraint. Groaning deeply under his breath, he rolled to pin one of her slender legs to the bed with his knee, and smoothed the T-shirt up to expose her body to his gaze. Dropping his head, he moved his mouth with hungry skill over her breasts, his tongue dampening the sensitive curves, his lips and teeth nipping and sucking with mounting urgency. Convulsing beneath him, she caught her fingers in his thick dark hair, arching involuntarily to offer the swell of her breasts more totally to his caresses.

'You have a very beautiful body,' he breathed softly, moulding the narrow indent of her waist with his hands, and slipping his fingers beneath her buttocks to splay her thighs, opening her tender secrets to his lidded gaze. 'I don't think I have ever wanted to make love to any woman as much as I want you, right now...'

'Oh...*oh*...!' The breathless exclamation of apprehension and delight made him laugh huskily, as he lowered his dark head to her flat, quivering stomach, then moved lower to the silky juncture of her legs to stroke his tongue boldly along the damp scented sweetness of her. 'Oh, Rick, please...'

'Gabriella...?' It was a hoarse question, and in response she opened herself further, colour dancing against her closed eyelids as the pleasure sensations climbed higher. He moved his mouth with agonising leisure back up the curves and hollows of her body, to slip his tongue around the acutely sensitive contours of her ear. Shuddering helplessly, desire outstripping reason, she moved to press herself against him, wriggling and frantically fumbling with the zip of his shorts, pushing his clothes impatiently away from the hardness of his body. His Bermuda shorts seemed to be impossible to remove. As she struggled with them, with trembling fingers, the sight of his arousal took her so much by surprise that she felt the shy colour surge into her face.

'Is flu an aphrodisiac, I wonder?' His teasing was husky, as he took over from her ineffectual attempts and dispensed with his clothes with minimum effort. Caressing the silky length of her body, he gave another half-groan, catching her against him. She could feel her heart thudding desperately against his hard chest, and even more intensely disturbing the heavy, hard jut of his sex against the tender warmth of her stomach.

'Oh, yes, sweetheart...' he groaned thickly, forcing a place for himself between her legs, raking his hands hungrily down her back to lift her against him, slipping demanding fingers into the hot, honeyed sweetness of her. 'I want you, I want to be so deep inside you...'

As the heavy, unfamiliar invasion went a step further, Gabriella caught her breath involuntarily. Her slight tension and the unmistakable resistance of her muscles, her slight withdrawal, her involuntary shiver of uncertainty communicated itself to him without words. There was a sudden stillness in him, a suspension of action. Then, slowly, with commendable restraint, he pulled away from her, his breathing shallow and laboured, searching her flushed, apprehensive face with narrowed, unreadable eyes.

'Gabriella, *mignonne...*' he grated unsteadily, dropping a swift, hard kiss on her lips. 'You're a virgin. *C'est vrai*? Is it true?' His eyes were impossible to read, smoky gold with suppressed desire, lidded to mere slits of amber light in his dark face.

'I...' The breath left her in a rush, and she stared up at him, trapped between acute shyness and wildly burgeoning desire.

'Everyone has to start somewhere,' she whispered huskily. 'Rick, I want you...! Don't...don't you want me now?'

'Are you crazy?' Shaking his head, as if to clear cobwebs from his brain, he dropped his mouth to kiss her deeply, hungrily, as if he were starving. Then, abruptly, he moved away, rolling to lie on the bed beside her at a safe distance, his chest lifting and falling rapidly with the effort to control his breathing.

She watched him, dying inside, trembling all over with nerves, and anticlimax, and a dozen other emotions too churned-up to identify. She felt so confused that she hadn't the least idea what she was expected to do now. Finally, reaching determinedly to retrieve his clothes, he jack-knifed off the bed and began pulling on his shorts with swift, deft motions. His face was dark as he glanced across at her.

'Stop looking like at me like that, Gabriella!' he told her harshly. 'I want you. *Tu comprends*?

Do you understand that? I want you very much. I'll need an hour in a cold shower after this...'

Slowly, she shook her head. She couldn't believe he was leaving her like this, while she was feeling so heated and aroused and shivering with need. How could he be so brutal? Uncomprehendingly, she stared at him as he dragged on his shirt, zipped his shorts with an air of bleak finality.

'Then why...?' she croaked helplessly, mortified beyond belief. Snatching her T-shirt, she hauled it quickly over her head, and hugged it around herself defensively. 'Why have you rejected me?' she finished up, with painful simplicity.

'*Dieu*!' he exploded. 'I'm not the one to take your virginity! It needs a special kind of relationship, Gabriella, to give yourself to someone for the first time. We don't have that kind of relationship...'

'What? What kind of relationship are you talking about?' she cried, choking on tears. 'I thought I had that with Piers! But I didn't! But with you I——'

'You hardly know me,' he reminded her, his deep voice abruptly gentle. 'Two nights marooned together in a double bed doesn't make a lasting liaison, Gabriella. Especially when one partner is delirious with the flu half the time!'

Stunned, she just gazed at him. She was too shocked and upset even to cry. Her throat felt tight, her stomach in knots. 'Rick...'

'Besides, I had no right taking advantage of you in the state you're in,' he cursed softly, glaring at her from beneath darkly drawn eyebrows, pushing a slightly unsteady hand through his tousled hair. '*Dieu*, Gabriella, I'm sorry! Can't you see I'm being cruel to be kind, you little idiot? I don't even know how it all happened...'

'How all *what* happened?' she echoed bitterly, turning to bury her face in the pillow. She hated herself for the emotional scene she was causing. She hardly recognised herself. Was this what falling in love did to your pride and self-control? Falling in love? Heaven help her, had she fallen in love with Rick Josephs, then...?

Dragging shuddering, sobbing breaths into her lungs as she fought for control, she said in a muffled voice, 'Nothing happened except that you succeeded in humiliating me. Was this revenge, because you thought I despised you?'

'*Ecoute*, Gabriella, I had no intention of humiliating you.'

He took a step towards her, then stopped. His face was a grim mask, his voice hardening. 'I am very flattered that you wanted me to be your first lover,' he continued softly, 'but when you're thinking straight you'll thank me for refusing the offer.'

She didn't look round. After a few moments, there was the rattle of the tray being reloaded, then the click of the door closing. He'd gone.

She turned on to her back, and stared at the ceiling fan. The blades were slowly rotating, with hypnotic regularity. Dazed, drained, she watched it until a degree of calm crept into her agitated mind.

She couldn't believe what had just happened. And even when she could, she couldn't make sense of it, of her own abrupt plunge into frantic sexual need. No, not just sexual need, emotional need. If sexual need were all it required to entice her to make love with someone, she'd have slept with Piers months ago...

But she simply couldn't make sense of the way Rick Josephs had made her feel, when Piers had done similar things without arousing so much as a palpitation in her heart...

Hectic colour burned her cheeks all over again as she relived the intimacy she'd just shared with Rick. It wasn't true to say that Piers had done similar things. She'd never shared that extent of abandoned lovemaking with Piers, never allowed him to take such unthinkable liberties with her body, during the whole of their engagement. So how could she have been so convinced she loved Piers, wanted to marry him?

Shell-shocked with the turmoil of emotion, she squeezed her eyes shut again. Being in Rick's arms, being touched by him, touching him, had made her feel an overpowering urge to get closer, closer physically, closer spiritually...

It made no sense. That was the only conclusion she could reach. She fell asleep again, her dreams broken and incomplete, but centring solely on a tall, dark-haired man with warm amber eyes...

If recovery meant feeling some physical strength returning, she was recovered, Gabriella reflected, waking again to find the sun shimmering through the bamboo blind. Slowly, her heart leaden but her legs a little more functional, she got up and found some clothes. The khaki shorts and the slept-in batik T-shirt seemed the best bet. Finding a hairbrush in her raffia bag, she untangled her hair with painful determination, and then plaited it into a thick blonde rope down her back. Her small make-up mirror revealed dark shadows under her eyes and an unhealthy-looking pallor to her cheeks. Not a pretty sight, she told herself, with a return to her old sense of humour. No wonder Rick changed his mind about making love to her...

Emerging into the sitting-room, she found him sprawled on a cane chair on the veranda. He wore dark glasses, and there was a glass of orange juice beside him, a book in his hands. Approaching on bare, silent feet, with her heart in her mouth, she stopped a few feet away, gazing at him, her heart contracting in an anguished stab of self-knowledge . . .

She loved him. Or if she didn't love him, if it was too early for it to be love, then she was wildly, deeply infatuated with him. The emotion she felt for him was stronger, more alarming and consuming than anything she'd ever felt for anyone before.

How she could feel like this she had no idea. How could she fall in love with a man who gave some indication of leading a dissolute, immoral lifestyle to rival Piers's, a man who'd just firmly rejected her feminine charms in bed, a man who seemed to do nothing but taunt her and make mocking remarks?

'Hello . . .' She cleared her throat nervously, and he turned his head slowly in response.

'*Salut,*' he murmured, not moving. 'I came in with some coffee about half an hour ago, but you were fast asleep.'

'Thanks, anyway.' She hesitated again, then went to sit on a nearby chair, shielding her eyes from the brilliance of the sun. The scene beyond the veranda was one of semi-devastation. Trees lay uprooted, branches and debris littered the beach. 'It looks like the aftermath of war out there.'

'There'll be no shortage of wood for cool winter nights,' he agreed expressionlessly, standing up. 'What can I get you, Gabriella?'

'My...' She swallowed jerkily, and tried again, fixing a bright smile on her mouth. 'My friends call me Gaby. Could...could we be friends, Rick? Nothing else, just friends...?'

There was a longish pause, as he stared back at her. Finally he removed his dark glasses, eyeing her with an impenetrable gaze. A flicker of humour softened his mouth.

'I'd be honoured, Gaby.' The trace of mockery was so faint as to be negligible, she decided courageously, growing in confidence. 'Do you want something to eat?' he added calmly. 'There are some prawns, and some cold chicken tikka.'

She shook her head. 'Maybe later. I'll get myself some fruit juice...'

'No. I'll get it. Sit still.'

She knew that note in his voice now. She stayed in the chair, without further argument. When he returned with the glass, she gathered all her remaining poise together. 'I had the weirdest dream,' she said with a short laugh. 'I dreamt I practically threw myself at you, begged you to make love to me!'

'Gabriella——' he began, a warning note in his voice.

'Gaby,' she reminded him calmly.

His eyes narrowed. 'Gaby, I——'

'Can you believe such a ridiculous dream?' she pressed on determinedly. 'I've got a feeling it was the result of all that delirium. I remember having tonsilitis as a child, hallucinating like mad. I used to think I was fighting armies of tiny little gnomes, who were hopping around all over my wardrobe and dressing-table——'

'Gaby, will you stop drivelling about hopping gnomes and listen?'

'No, you listen,' she cut in unevenly. 'I just wanted to say that if, by *any* chance, my dream...wasn't a dream...' She ignored the derisive glitter in his eyes and forged on, 'If I really *did* beg you to make love to me, then I apologise! I was...demented...'

'Sleep-walking?' he suggested drily, amusement softening his face. 'Gaby, you're apologising again. For something which wasn't your fault. What in the name of black *hell* did this monster Piers do to you?'

Shocked into silence, she stared at him. 'What do you mean?' It was an uncertain whisper. The searching gleam in Rick's narrowed gaze was unsettling. 'What do you mean, what did he *do* to me?'

'What kind of a relationship did you have with him?' he demanded impatiently. Pulling his chair closer to hers, he sat down and fixed her with a look which seemed to defy evasion.

'I...we were engaged,' she said flatly. Sipping the juice, she tasted the tang of citrus fruit, and pineapple, and some other exotic flavour. She savoured the taste, trying to capture the peace of this tiny island paradise to boost her morale and calm her nerves. Breathing in the sweetly scented

PLAY THE
LUCKY
CARNIVAL WHEEL
and get as many as
SIX FREE GIFTS..

HOW TO PLAY:

1. With a coin, carefully scratch away the silver panel opposite Then check your number against the numbers opposite to find out how many gifts you're eligible to receive.

2. You'll receive brand-new Mills & Boon Romances and possibly other gifts - ABSOLUTELY FREE! Return this card today and we'll promptly send you the free books and the gifts you've qualified for!

3. We're sure that, after your specially selected free books. you'll want more of these heartwarming Romances. So unless we hear otherwise, every month we will send you our 6 latest Romances for just £1.90 each * - the same price in the shops. Postage and Packing are free - we pay all the extras!
* Please note prices may be subject to VAT.

4. Your satisfaction is guaranteed! You may cancel or suspen your subscription at any time, simply by writing to us. The free books and gifts remain yours to keep.

NO COST! NO RISKS!
NO OBLIGATION TO BU

FREE! THIS CUDDLY TEDDY BEAR!

You'll love this little teddy bear. He's soft and cuddly with an adorable expression that's sure to make you smile.

PLAY THE LUCKY
"CARNIVAL WHEEL"

Scratch away the silver panel. Then look for your number below to see which gifts you're entitled to!

YES! Please send me all the free books and gifts to which I am entitled. I understand that I am under no obligation to purchase anything ever. If I choose to subscribe to the Mills & Boon Reader Service I will receive 6 brand new Romances for just £11.40 every month (subject to VAT). There is no charge for postage and packing. I may cancel or suspend my subscription at anytime simply by contacting you. The free books and gifts are mine to keep in anycase. I am over 18 years of age.

MS/MRS/MISS/MR _____

ADDRESS _____

_____ POSTCODE _____

SIGNATURE _____

5A4R

41	WORTH 4 FREE BOOKS, A FREE CUDDLY TEDDY AND FREE MYSTERY GIFT.
29	WORTH 4 FREE BOOKS AND A FREE CUDDLY TEDDY.
17	WORTH 4 FREE BOOKS.
5	WORTH 2 FREE BOOKS.

mps
MAILING PREFERENCE SERVICE

MORE GOOD NEWS FOR SUBSCRIBERS ONLY!

When you join the Mills & Boon Reader Service, you'll also get our free monthly Newsletter; featuring author news, horoscopes, competitions, special subscriber offers and much, much more!

Mills & Boon Reader Service
FREEPOST
P.O. Box 236
Croydon
Surrey
CR9 9EL

air of the island, the fragrance stronger after the storm, she could detect the mingled, subtle smell of ocean and pine trees and the rich, heady perfume of tropical flowers.

'Engaged for how long?'

'Four months...'

'Four months?' Rick's expression was incredulous. 'And you never made love?'

'Is that so shocking?' she countered, defensively. She reddened slightly under his probing scrutiny. He was shaking his head mockingly.

'Not shocking, Gaby sweetheart. Just unbelievable. Knowing what I now know about you.'

'Rick, that's not fair...' she began faintly, her heart starting to thud at the look in his eyes.

'But yes, it is fair,' he told her softly. 'You have a passionate nature, Gaby. So tell me why you were going to marry a man you didn't find sexually attractive.'

The colour receded from her face.

'That's not true. I loved him. At least, I thought I loved him...' Confused by her own feelings, she dropped her eyes from his.

'So what went wrong?'

'Oh, everything...' It was still so difficult to talk about it, she felt herself become tense all over.

'You discovered that you didn't love him?'

'I discovered...' She drew a deep breath. 'I found out he was sleeping with another woman.'

There, it was said. A sick feeling invariably overcame her whenever she spoke about it.

'While he was engaged to marry you?' Rick clarified, an edge of steel hardening his voice.

She nodded stiffly. 'She was also a friend. An older woman I'd worked with in my previous job. I'd trusted her. As for Piers ... all through my teens, I foolishly idolised him,' she confessed in a rush. 'His family and mine were friendly. Well, our mothers were friendly. Via the London charity circuit, mainly. Actually my mother was the dogsbody who did all the spadework; Piers's mother was the society lady who had all the moneyed contacts to pay hundreds of pounds for tickets to fashion shows and charity balls ... we were more than comfortably off, but they were very wealthy. They had so much money, they never really had to struggle for anything. Piers was the product of that, I suppose. Whatever he wanted, he got ...'

'And what line is Piers in?'

'Publishing. Magazines. It was indirectly through contacts of his that I got the job with *First Flair* ...'

There was a long, speculative silence.

'Would this by any chance be Piers Wellington?' Rick asked finally, very softly. 'Bertrand Wellington's son, of the Wellington Publishing Group?'

She stared at him in mounting horror. The chance of Rick actually *knowing* Piers had never occurred to her until now. Although, with Rick's friendship with Ursula Taylor, *First Flair's* fashion editor, she should surely have had the intelligence to have considered the possibility...

'You know him?'

'Not well,' he said thoughtfully, leaning back in his chair and crossing strong, stretched-out legs at the ankle. 'But enough to know that the man is a cold-blooded little bastard.'

'Well, that's it,' she felt compelled to add, as the pause lengthened uncomfortably. 'The story of my disastrous personal life to date. The bad news is that *First Flair* is up for sale, according to the grapevine, and the Wellington Group are very interested. I've been on tenterhooks ever since I heard the rumours—I shall probably end up on the dole!'

'I wouldn't lose any sleep over the Wellingtons buying *First Flair* and throwing you out of your job, Gabriella,' he murmured enigmatically. 'What I cannot understand is how you agreed to marry that little jerk in the first place.'

Gabriella sighed shakily. 'It was a combination of things. My mother was totally set on the idea...'

She caught the derisive glitter in his eyes, and made a face. 'Yes, I know. It sounds weak, a feeble reason. But you'd have to meet my mother to understand. Since she'd devoted the best part of her life to the fringes of rich society, the glimpse of "greater things" was more than she could resist...'

'*Entendu.*' He smiled faintly. 'What were the other things?'

'Sorry?'

'The other factors in this combination?' he prompted softly.

'Oh...as I said, I'd had a silly crush on him when I was younger. He was four years older, the distant, glamorous, golden boy, unattainable, someone to be looked up to and yearned after. The problem was, the more I got to know him, the less I could imagine being married to him...' She hesitated, glancing at Rick uncertainly. 'Does that sound terribly fickle?'

'No. Not fickle. But very young. Very...immature.'

'I was twenty,' she said tightly. 'We all make mistakes. You must have made a few in your life. Or do you, like Piers, consider yourself totally perfect, Rick?'

His gaze narrowed ominously. 'I've noticed that you do that when you're backed into a corner, Gabriella,' he drawled softly.

'Do what?'

'Go on the attack, in order to defend yourself.'

'I probably do. I have dozens of dreadful faults, I'm afraid. Unlike some people, who are paragons of every virtue...'

'Gabriella...or may I still call you Gaby?' he queried, eyeing her indignation with an air of amused tolerance. 'My own sins are not disputed. To claim I have led a life of purity and piety would be sadly deceiving, *ma petite*.'

'Please don't patronise me!' she burst out. 'I hate it when you treat me as if I'm young enough to be your... your *daughter*, or something...'

He raised a sardonic eyebrow. 'If I am guilty of it now, I cannot be accused of treating you like that a little earlier, Gaby.'

'No... but...' She stopped herself from going on, abruptly conscious of the narrow golden gaze assessing her from head to toe, and lingering on the curves in between. A warmth erupted somewhere in the region of her womb, an ache as old as time, powerful and pervasive. She shivered, hugging her arms round herself.

'Anyway,' she heard herself saying with a light bitterness, 'Piers evidently isn't the only one who prefers older women.'

'What is that supposed to signify, Gabriella?'

'I mean...' She swallowed with a sudden tremor of apprehension at the glint in his eyes. 'You and Ursula Taylor. I mean, whatever you might say, no one barges into someone's room like that if they're not on intimate terms with them!' It was excruciatingly painful to make the accusation again. She didn't even want to think about the possibility...

'You've got me all worked out, haven't you? Based on your cynical disillusionment at the ripe old age of twenty,' he mocked softly. 'But now, at least, I understand.' His mouth twisted as he stared into her flushed face. 'At last, I now see where this jaundiced, prejudiced outlook of yours gets its inspiration, *mignonne*. You judge everyone by the standards of your disastrous relationship with Piers Wellington. And only when you work that disillusionment out of your system, Gabriella, will you come even close to being ready for another relationship!'

CHAPTER SIX

AN UNEASY truce prevailed for the rest of the day. Gabriella found that while her temperature was virtually back to normal she was still weak and shaky. She felt too drained for much activity. Rick, giving no sign of frustration at their enforced stay, calmly donned swimming-trunks, extracted diving gear from a store at the rear of the *campement*, and disappeared underwater along the coral reef. The sun blazed down again from a deep blue sky dotted with white cotton-wool clouds. Gabriella, in her dried-out white sundress, lazed in a luxuriously padded lounger on the sugar-white beach under a big turquoise umbrella, idly watching the water for Rick's reappearance, and wondering when rescue, in the shape of the big wide world, would appear on the horizon to intrude on the enclosed intimacy of their situation.

She wasn't sure if she wanted this strange episode to come to an end. Was she a masochist? she wondered grimly. Could she actually enjoy being trapped in Rick's company, after the embarrassment between them? But he was *good* company, she reflected despairingly. He was relaxed, and witty, and thoughtful, and funny...

'I wish I could dive with you,' she said lightly, as Rick waded from the shallows, impressively tanned and lean and glistening with water. No man had any right to look so blatantly gorgeous, Gabriella decided, with bitter humour.

'Another time, maybe. I wouldn't risk it yet.'

'It's so unfair.' She gave a short laugh. 'Marooned at my leisure, feeling like death warmed up!'

'But my island is not a bad place to be recovering from flu, is it?' Rick grinned, dripping water on her as he heaved the aqualung from his shoulders, and subsided on to the chair beside her.

'Maybe not,' she conceded, 'but it's a lousy place to *have* flu.'

He levelled a veiled glance at her. 'Feeling sorry for yourself?' he teased. 'I wouldn't have classed you the self-pitying type, Gaby.'

'If I want to wallow in self-pity, that's my business.' She grinned faintly, wriggling involuntarily beneath the searching golden gaze. 'Besides, I haven't just lain here all afternoon, I've been "playing house", as I promised, remember?'

His eyes narrowed in amusement, he studied her face. 'Have you now?' he murmured.

'I've been using my creative talents with what's left in the fridge,' she confirmed, blushing faintly under the glittering appraisal. 'After all, you've

already scored points with that amazing con-
coction of yours...'

'I hadn't realised we were scoring points off
each other,' he pointed out, 'but if you've
managed to prepare a ten-course banquet, Gaby,
I'm not complaining. There's enough pure French
blood in my veins to give food high priority in
my personal scheme of things.'

'A ten-course banquet is going a bit far,' she
warned ruefully, as they walked back up to the
house. 'It's more of a starter, really...'

She'd discovered a white tablecloth in a drawer,
laid the table on the veranda. A glass-domed
green candle in the centre lent it an added air of
elegance. With a teaspoon as a scoop, she'd
transformed the canteloupe melon into bite-sized
balls, then mixed them with the remainder of the
prawns and a mayonnaise and lemon-juice
dressing.

'I thought we could finish up the chicken tikka
afterwards,' she explained, getting the melon
mixture out of the fridge to serve on lettuce-lined
dishes.

'Very pretty,' Rick admired with a grin, as they
sat down to eat. She'd laid out wine glasses, and
he looked at her questioningly as he fetched a
bottle of red wine. 'Is it safe to drink? You're
not planning to ply me with food and alcohol
and have your wicked way with me, are
you, Gaby?'

In spite of her struggle for poise, she found herself reddening.

'Rick...!' It was a faint, appalled protest. 'How can you be so...*foul*?'

'And how can you be so naïvely easy to tease, Gaby?' he mocked gently, uncorking the wine with a deft movement and pouring some of the deep red liquid into both glasses. 'If I have to watch every word I say from now on, then let's hope our rescuers arrive before nightfall!'

His wry taunt sank in. Declining further comment, she concentrated on eating. Her appetite hadn't fully returned, but the delicate flavours were irresistible. She heard herself making polite, automatic responses to Rick's easy dinner-table conversation, but his mention of rescue had made her uneasily conscious of the two alternative endings to this ironic little idyll. Either a boat or helicopter arrived before the sudden tropical darkness at seven p.m., or they were destined for another night here together...

Their rescuers were welcome to appear as soon as possible, she told herself coldly. But her heart squeezed in silent, yearning protest. She felt like a hopeless addict, impossibly hooked on his company. Even though his relationship with Ursula Taylor had never been fully explained, he'd long ago stopped reminding her in any way of Piers. There was a warmth and humour in Rick that Piers had always lacked. Rick seemed happy to laugh at life, to take things casually at face value. He was prone to mockery and teasing sarcasm, but he was brave and fearless and basically kind, strongly protective. He'd shown that when he'd looked after her while she was ill, and to her chagrin he'd demonstrated it even more clearly when he'd rejected her this morning...

Deep in her reverie, she shivered slightly, her stomach contracting at the memory. They might only have met a couple of days ago, she might know virtually nothing about him, but already she felt ridiculously dependent on him. Was this the way a hostage felt towards her captor? she wondered irrationally. Underlying distrust, blurred by a powerful emotional link?

She gave herself a violent mental shake, blinking her eyes to dilute the force of her thoughts. Her imagination was still addled by the after-effects of the fever, she reflected impatiently. She wasn't a hostage. Rick wasn't her captor. They'd been thrown together since her arrival in Mauritius by a series of unrelated incidents, and this latest situation was largely of her own making. If she hadn't pestered to be brought out here, they would never have been caught up in the cyclone, never have been stranded here in a small *campement* for two nights while she fought off the flu, never have been thrown together to the extent of this morning's humiliating eruption of desire...

'If you frown like that all evening, you'll have wrinkles before bedtime,' Rick told her coolly. 'Have some more wine, and relax, Gaby.'

'Sorry, I...' Glancing down at the horizon, where the sky met the ocean, she realised that the sun was setting, in a brilliant wash of purple and apricot. In a few minutes, it would be dark. And not a launch or a helicopter in sight. Her heart jolting, she said quickly, 'I was just wondering why no one has come out here to see how we are.' The small white lie was permissible in the circumstances, she told herself.

'Maybe they're too busy checking on a few thousand other stranded people.' Rick looked unconcerned, helping them both to more chicken. 'Don't worry, we'll survive another night if we have to.'

'I'll...I'll sleep on one of those sun-loungers,' she offered, stiffly.

Across the table, the golden eyes narrowed, the dark face hardening into cool male speculation. She felt her throat drying at the glinting, unreadable expression in his gaze.

'No. I'll do that,' he assured her flatly.

There was a brief, tense silence between them. Then, with an abrupt movement, he got up and went to get matches, returning to light the candle. As the darkness fell, the flickering glow brightened.

'I think there are some strawberries left,' he said, producing some from the recesses of the coolbox. 'Try some. They're small wild ones, grown all over the islands.'

'Thank you...' They were exquisitely flavoured. Eating the sweet fruit, and sipping wine, Rick's face a study of light and shadow across the table, she made a supreme effort to drag herself out of her introspection. Conversation took a more positive line. Rick proved knowledgeable about the latest films and books, both major interests of hers. He appeared to be a regular cinema-goer in New York, Paris or London, with a preference for off-beat, arty films, a penchant for Woody Allen. She discovered that they shared diverse tastes—a dislike of modern jazz, and a liking for heavy metal music, old Agatha Christie books, even the eccentric designs of the Spanish architect Gaudí.

'Speaking of architects,' she said suddenly, 'what about your plans for this house...when do you intend to start work on it?'

'I'm working on plans now, with an architect in Mauritius. I want to do it carefully, retain the traditional look,' he told her thoughtfully. 'And I'm keen to protect the wildlife on the island too. I'm in no hurry—I'd rather get it right, and take my time over it.'

She nodded. 'I imagine it would be easy to rush through some hideous extension to this place, ruin the atmosphere. But don't you have other commitments? I mean, surely you can't have unlimited time to spend over here...?'

'I told you, I work for myself. I can spend time wherever I want, within reason...' He was watching her face, his expression veiled. 'Tell me more about your family, Gaby,' he said unexpectedly, his tone cool. 'You've mentioned your mother and that you're an only child—what about your father?'

'My father?' She felt surprised. 'I adore my father. He's a lovely man—quiet, very kind, very clever...'

'He certainly has a fan club in his daughter.' Rick grinned faintly. 'What does he do?'

'He's a doctor. A consultant surgeon. He specialises in children's ailments—ear, nose and throat.'

'Did he approve of your engagement to Piers Wellington?'

She was taken aback by the question. Considering it carefully, she finally shook her head.

'What a strange thing to ask,' she began. 'Why ask that?'

'Just curiosity. Did he approve, Gaby?'

'I...no. I don't think he did...at least, when I broke it off with Piers, he seemed pleased...'

She felt a stab of annoyance with him again, and realised why. 'You know, you're very good at pumping personal information out of people, Rick. And very good at avoiding giving any about yourself!'

There was a silence.

'OK. What do you want to know?' It was a lazy invitation. She blinked at him distrustfully.

'Are you...married?' She flinched at the gleam of laughter her question provoked.

'Not now.'

'You were?' she persisted doggedly. 'Are you divorced?'

'Yes,' he said flatly. 'Nine years ago.'

'What happened?'

He spoke slowly, thoughtfully. 'Quite early on in our brief marriage she discovered she'd married the wrong man...'

'Oh, I'm so sorry...'

'It's all right, Gaby, my ego took quite a knock at the time, but I assure you I'm over it now.'

His wife must have been either blind or mentally deficient, Gabriella thought privately. As if reading her thoughts, he added, 'It was as much my fault as hers. I was building up my career. I was away so much, she felt neglected. Sometimes these things happen. Particularly when people are too young to know any better. And in case you're wondering, I still believe in the sanctity of marriage as an institution.' His tone was wryly mocking. 'Are there any more questions to satisfy your inquisitive little mind?'

'What do you *do*?'

'Do?' He was mockingly blank.

'For a *living*!'

'I take photographs.'

Stunned, she stared at him. 'You're a photographer?' she said at last.

He grinned, leaning back in his chair. 'That's the name usually given to people who take photographs for a living.'

Reddening slightly, she controlled her temper. 'Must you always be so...sardonic? Are you a *fashion* photographer? Is...is that how you know Ursula Taylor?'

'Indirectly.'

Bewildered, she stared at him. He was a fashion photographer? Freelance? He knew Ursula through his work? She'd never come across his name, so he couldn't be very well-known and therefore very successful, and yet he appeared to be wealthy, and powerful, and highly confident, all the typical hallmarks of a successful professional man...

'How long have you been in the profession? Is Ursula finding work for you?'

'To answer in the same order, quite a few years, and no, I doubt it very much,' he replied calmly. 'Ursula Taylor and I have recently had a major disagreement.'

'Personally? Or professionally?'

'Personally.'

She waited, but he seemed in no hurry to expand. Anger was mounting. He'd watched her busily taking all her amateurish shots of locations on their tour—now she came to think of it he *had* calmly suggested the best angles or the most effective distances—but he'd said nothing about his own profession...how he must have secretly laughed at her bumbling attempts...

'Why on earth didn't you tell me you were a professional photographer? Knowing I work for *First Flair*... Are you *congenitally* secretive?' she exploded at last, unable to control her exasperation.

'Sadly, yes,' he laughed, watching as she sprang to her feet, began to collect the plates. 'Leave that, Gaby. I'll do it.' He stood up too, put a hand over hers, stopping her from her angry task. His touch was like a shot of adrenalin into her nervous system. She jumped involuntarily, but allowed herself to be propelled back into her chair.

'Would you like coffee? There's no milk left, but you can have it black.'

'No, thanks,' she snapped, too infuriated by his refusal to confide in her. She sensed he was deliberately withholding even more vital information about himself, and somehow it felt like a deliberate snub. She'd opened up to him, and he was just humouring her, keeping his own counsel, about things that really mattered... That hurt, more than anything she could currently think of. 'I've a good mind to go and build a fire on the beach, start sending smoke signals, anything to get me out of here!'

'There's probably plenty of firewood, but don't forget the *couleuvres*,' he teased unhelpfully.

'I *hate* you, Rick Josephs!'

'Such passion, so sadly misplaced.'

'I'm going to bed,' she told him shakily.

'Isn't it rather early?'

'No. I'm tired. I'll put the sun-lounger in the corner of the bedroom and I'll sleep on that...'

'Like hell you will.' He laughed shortly, catching hold of her arm as she went to get the chair from the side of the veranda. 'You need a good night's rest, Gaby. So stop stamping around in a temper, and go and get one.'

'I'm not sharing a bed with you!'

'You won't have to,' he told her flatly. 'I'll sleep on the damned sun-lounger. Satisfied?'

'No!' she half sobbed, marching for the bedroom. 'I'd rather be back in the freezing fog in London than spend another night in your company, even if we do have separate sleeping arrangements...'

'So what happened to our new friendship?' he mocked at her departing figure. 'I knew you were fickle, Gabriella.'

She slammed the bathroom door behind her, and stood for a long time beneath a soothing warm shower, fighting her emotions, and feeling appalled at her violent outburst.

In the middle of the night, she woke up. When her brain had managed to sort out where she was again, she realised sleepily that Rick had kept his promise. He must be sleeping on a sun-lounger, in the sitting-room. There was no sign of him in the bedroom.

She was emerging from the bathroom a few minutes later, when she felt the thing move at her feet. She looked down, horror prickling her skin. There was something narrow and shadowy on the dark flagstoned floor, slithering rapidly away from her towards the sitting-room.

With a startled shriek, she jumped almost a foot in the air before running, panic-driven, for the safety of the bed at such speed that she could have taken flight with the impetus. Seconds later, Rick appeared, finding her shuddering with reaction as he snapped on the lamp beside the bed.

'What's wrong? Another nightmare?'

'No, one of your Indian snakes ... !' she whispered, staring down at the floor fearfully.

Some of the tension faded from Rick's dark face.

'Is that all? I was afraid you were being murdered in your bed!' he grinned. 'Where did it go?'

'Into the sitting-room!'

He went in search of it, and she sat, goosepimples prickling her skin all over, hugging the sleeping-bag around herself in spite of the warmth of the night. When he came back, he had an air of triumph.

'I have escorted the offending snake outside,' he assured her gravely, coming to twist up her chin and inspect her white face. 'I told you, Gaby, they are harmless. Did the poor little creature attack you, trap you in a corner, spit poison venom at you?'

'No! it just...*slithered*!'

'That's the way snakes get around. They're built to slither.'

'I know that!' she told him through clenched teeth. 'Look, I accept that they're probably very charming, friendly little snakes, I was just startled, that's all! It made me jump...' she defended herself shakily.

'Then I'm sorry you were scared,' he said more gently. 'You're white, and shivering, *mignonne*.' He searched her face with a frown, sitting down on the bed, and drawing her against his chest in a comforting, brotherly gesture. 'Don't be frightened.'

Gradually the shivering slowed. In its place crept a trembling feeling of another kind.

'There is nothing here that will hurt you, Gaby.' Rick's voice was deeper, with a hoarser note which made her heart miss a beat.

'Isn't there?' she whispered, suddenly far more affected by his closeness than by the recent encounter with the snake. 'I'm not sure about that...'

'Gaby...' The grating warning in his voice made her heart begin to thud faster. But a warmth was flooding her as he held her in his arms. Much too fast, much too strongly, it was changing from warmth to heat, from heat to fire. This time there was no fever, nothing to confuse or detract from the flames of desire leaping into uncontrollable life between them, or the debilitating weakness creeping through her limbs.

'Rick...' She heard her own voice and hardly recognised it. It was a hoarse, hungry whisper as she wriggled against him in helpless need, tried and failed to stop her arms from going around him, felt her breasts tighten and peak against the warmth of his naked chest. In nothing but the white Bermudas, he was all lean, tanned muscle, potently, overwhelmingly male. A disturbing source of comfort and threat...

'Don't go...' Was that her voice again? Shamelessly urging him to stay, to hold her more tightly?

With a low, violent curse beneath his breath, he twisted her round and sought her soft mouth, kissing her hungrily, plunging his tongue with such restrained ferocity against hers that she felt the wild, urgent stab of response shivering through her.

'Stay, please, Rick...' she whispered chokingly, as he broke free and turned away. 'I love you...!'

The words were out, and, feeling fearfully vulnerable and exposed, she caught her breath in anguish. Slowly, he turned back to look at her, a pulse jumping in his cheek. There was no trace now of amusement, or teasing, or mockery in his hard features. Lost in the darkness of his eyes, she stared back.

'No. You don't love me, Gaby,' he told her roughly, his face a mask. 'You're too young to know the meaning of the word!'

'That's not true,' she whispered intensely. She felt too strung up for tears, too caught up in the bewildering urgency of the situation. 'Don't judge me by your ex-wife, Rick. That's not fair...'

'Gaby, *écoute-moi*,' he urged gently, the rise and fall of his chest betraying his emotion. 'You are very beautiful. With your dark green eyes and your long blonde hair and your...exquisite body you could have any man you wanted...but to make it last you need to grow up. You need to mature. Love can grow and change and get better between two people if they're mature enough, Gaby.'

'All I know is, I've never felt like this for anyone before,' she choked on a throat so tight that she could hardly breathe. 'I've never spoken like this to any man before! I don't know how else to get through to you—you're so...shuttered and secretive, but you do feel something for me, I can see it in your eyes...'

'You see me as a substitute for Piers Wellington,' he told her bluntly, controlling his breathing now, standing up and raking his hands impatiently through his dark hair. 'You thought you loved him, remember? Enough to wear his ring. Then you discovered he was sleeping with another woman. I think you're just trying to

-prove something to yourself, Gaby. And I'm not in the market for supplying the proof...'

Aghast, she stared at him wide-eyed.

'Doesn't the fact that I never wanted Piers to make love to me tell you anything?' she whispered, with simple honesty, her face burning with the fresh agony of rejection. 'I swear to you, Rick, I am old enough, and mature enough, to know exactly how I feel about you!'

There was a fraught, endless silence, while she sat trembling with tension on the bed. He stared at her with such fierce intensity that she felt as if he could see right into her soul.

'No, Gaby...' It was a grated denial.

'*Yes*!'

With a shiver of emotion, her eyes locked on his, she caught hold of the hem of her T-shirt, and ripped it up over her head, tossing it down on the bed like a gauntlet. Proud and naked, she endured the unblinking scrutiny for more long-drawn-out seconds. Then with a soft expletive he crossed to the bed, and came down beside her.

'Gaby...' He took her shoulders, giving her a slight, furious shake before folding her into his arms. 'You're crazy, *tu sais*? Crazy...'

'About you...' she choked, on a shaky laugh, tears stinging her eyelids as he trailed hungry, starving kisses from her parted lips to her cheekbones, temples, along the smooth curve of her forehead, down the tender arch of her neck.

'*Dieu*,' he muttered thickly, a degree of his control slipping as he dropped his mouth to the sweet, high thrust of her breasts, forcing her back against the pillow. '*J'en peux plus*, Gaby! I can't take any more...'

The weight of his body was sheer joy against hers. Lost to the wild emotion of the moment, she closed her eyes, wrapped her arms around the broad strength of his back. As he began his tender, skilful assault on her senses with mouth, and hands and body, she let her mouth seek the rough and the smooth of his skin, her tongue explore the tight hardness of small, flat nipples among their coarse sprinkling of dark hair, her fingers roam in mounting astonishment along the almost-familiar hollows and ripples of muscle and sinew.

'Oh, yes...' It was her own husky surrender, breathed against his mouth, hectic, mindless, seeking some unknown fulfilment which seemed to be the only reality in a world that was tipping and spinning way out of control. 'Oh, please, yes...Rick, yes...!'

She writhed, clutching him to her, the need to be closer seeming irrational as their bodies were already moulded together as tightly as possible. The feverish impatience engulfing her was abruptly matched by the powerful, devastating reaction in Rick.

'*Gaby*...!' The hot thrust of possession was a surge of pleasure and pain, the pain rapidly diminishing, until it was a faint, barely remembered part of the whole wondrous act of giving.

Arching beneath him, following his lead, swelling mysteriously with a coiled-up, nameless crescendo of need, she dug her nails unthinkingly into the flat plane of his shoulderblades, curled her legs around his waist, and cried his name in utter abandon as a micro-explosion seemed to take place inside her. The shock waves radiated in ever-widening ripples to delight every millimetre of her body.

'Oh...!' It was part sob, part laugh, part scream, as she tipped over some invisible edge of darkness and plunged deeper, deeper into ecstatic swirls of sensation.

'Gaby, sweetheart...' Rick's voice was thick and hoarse, raw with emotion against her lips as he felt her shudder in response. 'You're unbelievable...so sweet and tight, *mignonne*, like hot silk...!'

'*Rick*...!'

It was impossible, she thought dimly, her senses shimmering on the tip of the volcano, to feel any more...but then the stars burst, the world tipped and broke away from her and spun dizzyingly off into infinity and she was floating, weightless as air, in the slip-stream...

There was a voice, a disembodied voice. Through misty layers of consciousness, Gabriella fought her way up to the surface.

She was still closely entwined in Rick's arms,
her head in a tousled mop of blonde hair pil-
lowed on his chest, his hard warmth miracu-
lously locked with her softness, one muscular
forearm firmly trapping her against him. She
couldn't remember ever waking up to such an
overwhelmingly wonderful feeling...

But it was morning. There was daylight again,
the sun slanting through the blind, the bedroom
full of dancing dust-motes in the stripes of light.
And there was the voice, more clearly now.
Stirring in Rick's arms, Gabriella was suddenly,
abruptly wide awake. Blinking and focusing on
the doorway, she stiffened in dismay.

'So *this* is where you're hiding, Gabriella.'

Ursula Taylor stood there, paler and thinner
after her flu, bone-thin and elegant in a strappy
black sundress, glossy dark hair cascading down
her back, cigarette in hand, her heavy-lidded eyes
missing nothing as she studied the scene.

'I was told at the hotel that Patrick was busy
playing shipwrecks on his own private island.' She
gave a short, husky, far from humorous laugh.
'But now I know better—he's far busier dis-
rupting my fashion shoot by deliberately seducing my *naïve* little assistant!'

CHAPTER SEVEN

'URSULA...' As if from a great distance, Gabriella heard Rick's curt response, low and controlled but nevertheless steel-tipped. 'Get the hell out of here...!'

'When I've *retrieved* my assistant, I will!' Ursula hurled at him, her usual cool sophistication deserting her. 'Gabriella, I don't know if you think sleeping with the great Patrick St Josef is going to further your career, my dear, but I can assure you it will have the opposite effect as far as *First Flair* magazine is concerned! I'll see you down at my boat in five minutes!'

'Gaby's going nowhere,' Rick said bluntly, 'until we sort this out. Go back to Mauritius, Ursula, and stay there!'

'Gabriella?' Ursula's voice rose in mounting anger, and, white-faced, Gabriella sat slowly up in bed, the sleeping-bag clutched against her.

Her brain wouldn't work. She felt numb with shock. If only this could be another bad dream, another nightmare... but it seemed all too real. Rick said something to her, but she couldn't take it in. All she could hear were Ursula's words. All she could think of was that Rick had lied to her about his name...

Deliberately lied to her about his identity.

Slowly, tense with embarrassment and confusion, she turned her head to stare at the dark-faced stranger beside her in bed. Rick Josephs was... Patrick St Josef? The great and famous Patrick St Josef, international photographer, sought after by actresses, pop stars and British and European royalty to have their photographic portraits taken?

Her heart plummeted crazily in her chest. Heat crept into her face, seemed to burn all over her body. No wonder he'd been treating her with such patronising amusement ever since they'd met! A naïve, ignorant little twenty-one-year-old with a lowly job and lofty ambitions. She must have kept him vastly entertained...

Swinging his legs calmly out of the bed, Rick had grabbed his shorts and hauled them on. Now he was standing up in an uncoiling of rock-hard muscle and taut, darkly tanned flesh to confront Ursula's furious figure. The older woman took an involuntary step back towards the door.

'How *could* you, Patrick?' she snarled, becoming flushed in the face as she stared at his blatant masculinity. 'Even if you were angry with me, how could you deliberately disrupt *First Flair*'s assignment, side-track Gabriella, encourage her to waste her time here with you, when——?'

'Allow me to escort you off my island, Ursula.' The drily amused suggestion was softly spoken and more daunting because of it. 'I assume you've come independently? You're not the rescue party?'

'The marina said they were sending some mechanic out in your helicopter, in case you needed any repairs to your boat,' she snapped furiously. 'But I couldn't wait around for them to move themselves into action! I've got a fashion shoot to organise, and my assistant seems to have found other things to occupy her mind!'

'Gabriella will come back to work when she's ready...'

'If you don't mind, I *can* speak for myself!' Gabriella, trembling with rage, found her voice at last, forcing herself to speak calmly, in her most businesslike tone. 'I...I'm sorry, Ursula! Of course I'll come back now! I've got lots of notes, and a whole roll of film I took during a tour of suitable locations...'

Far from appearing mollified, Ursula had swung back to stare furiously at Gabriella's strained white face.

'Oh, please don't tear yourself away from your little love nest, Gabriella! Perhaps *when* you're ready, you'll deign to come and tell me precisely what you feel you've achieved on *First Flair's* behalf?'

Swinging out of the room, Ursula slammed the door behind her with a crash which reverberated around the *campement*.

Taut with nervous tension, shaking all over, Gabriella abruptly galvanised herself into action, jumping out of bed, dragging on her T-shirt, preparing to follow, to try and explain.

'Wait, Gaby,' Rick advised with cool arrogance. Catching hold of her arm, he forcibly restrained her as she made a dive for the door. 'I know Ursula. Leave it until she's calmed down. You'll achieve nothing trying to talk to her when she's in this mood...'

'I'm sure you do *know* Ursula!' Gabriella couldn't help herself—the accusing words burst out unchecked. 'It's quite obvious, even to a half-witted little simpleton like me, that you and Ursula are more than merely *acquainted*!'

'Gabriella, you're over-reacting.'

Rick turned a cool, shuttered gaze on her, and as she tensed defensively there was a silence, dragging out unbearably, lengthening and tightening.

'Remember I said you jump to conclusions too easily?' The deep voice was wryly thoughtful, as if he was weighing up the situation, humouring her.

'Am I expected to believe what you tell me,' she demanded chokingly, 'when you haven't even been truthful about your real *name*?'

The enormity of her dilemma finally sank in. She squeezed her eyes shut in abrupt despair. This man was a world celebrity in the photography profession. And she was so naïve and inexperienced that she hadn't even recognised him! Worse still, last night she'd thrown herself at him, begged him to make love to her, told him she loved him. What a fool, what an *idiot* she'd made of herself!

The only way of retrieving the situation was to control her urge to collapse in tears, try to put a brave face on it. Perhaps even attempt to see the funny side. There had to be one. Assuming your sense of humour ran to the sick and masochistic...

'Whether I call myself Rick Josephs or Patrick St Josef, what difference does it make?' he queried wryly.

'No difference at all! Apart from entertainment value for you!'

The bitter sarcasm in her voice fell like drops of acid into the silence between them. Rick was very still. Suddenly his dark face was harsh and distant. She couldn't read his thoughts at all, she realised distractedly.

'Is that what you really believe?' he queried finally. His voice was rough, his eyes a deep, smoky gold as he watched her. 'That you were an evening's entertainment?'

'Yes...no...I don't know!' she managed in a taut, deceptively calm voice. 'But it doesn't matter anyway. Last night was my fault! I practically threw myself at you, didn't I?' She gave a short laugh, which choked on a tell-tale sob. 'It just goes to show a girl should be careful whom she throws herself at! You'd think, with my track record, I'd have known better...'

'Gabriella, you must know you're talking nonsense...' Rick sounded ominously calm and patient.

'No, I'm talking perfectly good sense. And by the way, I deeply object to you speaking to Ursula just now on my behalf! Just because we...we made love last night, it doesn't mean you *own* me!'

'Own you? Maybe not,' Rick mocked softly, his eyes on the soft uptilt of her breasts beneath the T-shirt before moving slowly back up to her tense face. 'But I reckon being the first man across the threshold, *mignonne*, gives me a fair proportion of shares.'

Jolted from her shaky composure into unexpected fury, she involuntarily lashed out at him. He caught her hand, fending the blow. His smile was grim.

'I don't agree with violence, Gaby.' The fingers restraining her were vice-like, despite his cool assurance.

'Of all the arrogant...!' Breathless, she struggled with all her strength, but she couldn't free her hand. Then her protest was abruptly halted as he dragged her forcefully into his arms, crushing his mouth over hers to silence her.

'Rick, leave me alone...!' she managed to gasp, when he freed her mouth at last.

'No way, Gaby,' he growled. 'You don't come on to a man the way you did last night, then switch on the stop-light in the morning...'

With this outrageously arrogant statement, Rick deepened the kiss, branding her with the sheer potency of his sexuality. Locked in the hard strength of his arms, in spite of her anger and confusion her emotions betrayed her, leaping and soaring to blot out the pain and rekindle the force of last night's passion...

'Rick, let me go...' she whispered, with less conviction. She was quivering involuntarily beneath his seeking, demanding hands. 'You'll get me sacked...I must go after Ursula...'

'Ursula can wait,' he muttered harshly, the glitter in his eyes annihilating her as he lifted her up in his arms and laid her back on the bed. 'This can't...'

His sensual assault held a barely restrained ferocity. To her shame, Gabriella responded, anger lending an edge to her emotions. The physical pleasure was almost a pain, but far greater and far more devastating was the emotional need. Lovemaking had little to do with the body after all, she reflected wildly, thinking of those failed attempts with Piers, of the essential ingredient lacking in their chemistry...

Rick's touch made her melt and surge and flood inside with warmth and yearning. As frantically and desperately as someone drowning in a whirlpool, she clung to him, drank in his kisses, writhed and arched into the hardness of his arms.

'Tell me you want me,' he breathed, shuddering above her as he scanned her flushed, hectic cheeks and bright, lidded eyes. 'Give me the honesty you gave me last night...'

'Give me one good reason why I should,' she whispered huskily, shivering as he prised open her soft thighs to accommodate his hard muscularity, tensing in panic-stricken alarm as reality returned just in time to save her from total submission. 'And what difference would it make?' she gasped, trembling and fighting to free herself. 'You're taking what you want in any case...!'

'Only because you want it too,' he murmured harshly, against her lips. 'You're just too confused to realise it...'

'No...*no*! I *don't* want it...!' His goading words were the last straw. This was madness, if she let him dominate her like this. Emotional suicide. This sudden knowledge gave her the strength to fight him with renewed determination, writhing with fierce urgency.

Abruptly, unexpectedly, she was free. Shaking with anger and hurt pride, she curled over on her side. Shame was invading every pore of her body.

If she'd allowed it to happen, she thought dimly, it would have been just like before. No, more so. Wilder, hotter, more gloriously, uncontrollably heavenly than the first time. How could she feel such depth of emotion for someone she didn't trust?

'Why did you do that?' she whispered at last.

'Do what?' he mocked softly. The deep voice was thicker, husky with suppressed desire. Something contracted deep inside her. Misery seemed to well from somewhere deeper still.

'Try to... to use sex as a smokescreen!'

'Is that what you think I was doing?' He sounded speculative. 'Maybe I wanted to reassure myself that last night really happened. That it wasn't just another erotic dream,' he mocked gently. 'And to prove something to you.'

She tensed, twisting back to look at him.

'Prove what an expert lover you are?' she suggested bitterly, levering herself up with an immense effort. 'Or prove you're more powerful than Ursula? Why do I feel as if I'm a pawn in some sick game you're both playing?'

'You're not a pawn in any game, Gaby. If you stop lashing out long enough, you'll begin to see that.'

'Forget it, Rick,' she said, her voice thick with tears. 'I don't want to hear any more lies. I told you, it doesn't matter anyway...'

He was lying on his back, his hands behind his head, watching her with that sphinx-like mask which devastated her defences. She couldn't speak again for a few moments, until she'd controlled the huge lump in her throat. When she had her emotions tightly in check, she managed a shrug and a passable attempt at a smile.

'I'm going to have a shower,' she announced with false brightness, standing up. 'And then I'm going to see if I can catch the next passing boat back to Mauritius! I'm sure there's a new jargon phrase to suit this situation, isn't there? "Damage limitation"? I'll see what I can salvage of my job with *First Flair*, and don't worry, now that I know what a famous celebrity I've been hobnobbing with I won't embarrass you in front of everyone by throwing myself at you again!'

'I'm deeply grateful for that consolation, Gabriella.'

Rick's face lacked expression as she risked one last glance at him. But his cool, ironic response echoed in her ears long after she'd left.

To say that her immediate future seemed bleak, Gabriella reflected with numb detachment, soaking in a lukewarm, magnolia-scented bath in her hotel room in the Sable Royale, was an understatement.

The initial urge to burst into endless tears and fall apart with grief and misery had been thankfully postponed. She might well do that in the sanctuary of her own little flat in London, or even in the more comforting sanctum of her father's private consulting-rooms. She definitely couldn't do it on her mother's shoulder. After the scant support she'd received over the Piers fiasco,

Gabriella had mentally consigned her mother, love her dearly as she might, to superficial conversations about hair, holidays and clothes.

But right now, stranded on a tiny island in the Indian Ocean courtesy of *First Flair's* expense account, and in deep trouble over her job, falling apart was a luxury she couldn't afford.

The problem was, it was all very well to say to Rick that she needed to salvage her job, limit the damage done. But how could she go on working for Ursula, now that that woman had discovered Rick in bed with her?

Stifling a groan of anguish, she closed her eyes tightly, trying to blot out the images. As long as she lived, she'd remember that nightmarish transition from ecstasy to reality. Waking in Rick's arms, with such a surge of joy in her heart, to find Ursula in the room, hurling accusations...

Miserably, she trailed her fingers through the bubbles in the bath.

There was no point yearning after Rick Josephs. Or Patrick St Josef, as she'd better get used to calling him. She'd pushed him into making love to her, hadn't she? He'd made it plain he didn't want to get involved. How had he put it? They didn't have that kind of relationship. They hardly knew each other. What happened had just been a result of their intimate confinement on the island. Their closeness in sharing a bedroom, and a bed...

Gabriella winced, as if she'd received a blow
to the stomach. Emotionally, she was hurting
inside, so badly that it was like a physical pain.
Sinking her teeth into her lower lip, she forced
herself to think of something else. But all she
found herself doing was comparing the whole
ghastly mess with the disaster over Piers. And
that wasn't fair either. First, because she now
knew she'd never loved Piers. Being with Rick
had opened her eyes to how it felt to be deeply,
passionately in love. To feel desired, to feel so
obsessed by a man that surrendering her body
was the most natural thing in the world...

And then, Rick's behaviour might have been
callous, but it came nowhere near the selfish
cruelty of Piers's actions. She opened her eyes
and retrieved the circular peach-coloured soap
from the bathwater, distractedly lathering it in
her hands until they were coated in creamy
bubbles. Switching her mind from the painful
contemplation of Rick's behaviour, she found
herself thinking instead of her engagement to
Piers.

They'd been seeing each other for about six
months before they became engaged, going out
to dinner at expensive restaurants, to theatres and
West End musicals, attending dinner parties in
the sophisticated circle Piers moved in so much
more effortlessly than she'd ever done. Although
Piers was only four years older, he'd always
seemed much more worldly-wise. And yet, be-

cause of working for his powerful father in the family business, he'd spent his whole life getting what he wanted easily, automatically. Subconsciously, she must have been aware all along of inner reservations about their relationship. But her teenage admiration for him had lingered on. She had truly thought she was in love with him. The only tell-tale signs of something wrong had been her lack of real response to his lovemaking. And she'd thought that was her fault. Her strict boarding convent had done little to prepare her for the realities of sex. She'd been worried that she was frigid. Anything heavier than kissing had triggered a tense apprehension which Piers had found at first amusing, and then increasingly infuriating...

Then, out of the blue, he'd asked her to marry him, without prior warning of his intention, at a family Christmas dinner.

She'd felt sure their mothers had been behind it. Presented with a sparkling diamond ring, she'd felt overwhelmed by it all, the congratulations and the tearful toasts, Piers gazing at her with a rather smug air of proud ownership. Looking back, it struck her that he'd looked as if he'd just acquired a desirable object, like a piece of furniture or a new car.

Over the next few months, the sensation had intensified. She had been paraded around as a decorative appendage. When Piers had rung to arrange some social event, she had been told what to wear, how to do her hair, even what to say to his important business colleagues. After a while, the last vestiges of her teenage crush on him had evaporated in the knowledge that she didn't love him, that she'd made a terrible mistake in accepting that surprise diamond ring at that family party.

Her guilt had been increased by feelings of inadequacy in their sexual relationship. Whenever Piers had showed signs of wanting more, she'd frozen up inside, begged him for more time. Shortly after their engagement, Piers had made it clear that in buying her the ring he'd expected to put an end to her ridiculous inhibitions. He had lost his patience, one night, and tried to force her. Fighting him off, frightened and appalled, a bitter argument had erupted. Shattered, but clearer in her mind about her true feelings for him, she'd returned his ring.

And then, from a mutual friend, she'd found out about the other woman in Piers's life. She'd discovered that Piers had been having a long-standing sexual relationship with someone else, all the time he'd been engaged to her. It had been someone from Gabriella's previous job with a PR company: a woman a few years older, someone she'd trusted, thought of as a friend...

No, it really wasn't fair to liken Rick to Piers. Rick might have deceived her over his true identity, and he might be somehow involved with Ursula Taylor, which hurt more than she cared to acknowledge, but he hadn't deliberately set out to woo her, and then deceive her, as Piers had done. Had he?

No. She couldn't, wouldn't believe that. He'd shown that he was thoughtful and caring, while they were on his island together. He'd shown that he desired her, but when he realised she was a virgin he'd been protective, he'd refused to take advantage ... he'd only made love to her because she'd wanted him to...

With a jerk of self-awareness, she stopped short. She stared despairingly at her soapy hands, her heart thumping in her chest, her throat contracting. Why was she making allowances for him, castigating herself like this? Wasn't she just grasping at straws, desperate for proof that the man she'd fallen in love with hadn't deliberately, intentionally set out to shatter her illusions in this way...?

She felt sick and dizzy with the effort. She was going round and round in mental circles. She'd go mad. Leave it. Forget it. What was done was done, as her father would say. Water under the bridge. Learn by the experience.

There was a sharp knocking on her bedroom door. Wrapping herself in a big white bathrobe, she opened the door to find Ursula standing there, dark hair swept up in a top-knot, model-slim in a short navy blue silk dress. Her carefully made-up face projected cool hostility. In her hand, she held the notes Gabriella had given her, and a wallet of photographs.

'Sorry to drag you out of the bath, Gabriella——' she managed to sound the opposite '—but I've had a look through these notes of yours, and I've had your photographs developed. Can I come in a moment?'

With a nod, Gabriella stood back to allow the other woman into the room.

'I was quite impressed,' Ursula informed her, sauntering to the balcony and sitting down in one of the cane chairs. It was mid-afternoon, and the beach was dotted with huge discs of black shade from the thatched sun-parasols. Wind-surf sails made splashes of colour against the silvery blue and green. 'You've done quite a good job after all!'

Gabriella tried hard to hide her astonishment. 'Thank you. Can...can I get you something to drink?'

'No. This isn't precisely a friendly social call, Gabriella.' Ursula's eyes were her most arresting feature, a piercing shade of ice-blue. Gabriella felt her heart sink at the uncompromising expression she detected there.

'I see...' She cleared her throat and took the plunge. 'Look, Ursula, I'm sorry about what happened with Rick...'

'Patrick,' the dark woman corrected coldly. 'And you needn't bother making excuses. I can quite understand your temptation, my dear. Most girls feel the same way about Patrick St Josef. And, with a man and woman thrown together like that, most men would be incapable of resisting the opportunity to take full advantage. However, it would be extremely naïve of you to read anything more into it. I advise you to stay away from him during the rest of your stay in Mauritius. If you want to keep your job.'

Gabriella stared at her with mounting disbelief.

'Are you telling me I'm sacked if I talk to Rick again?' she queried, as politely as she could.

'Don't be melodramatic, Gabriella.' The older woman eyed her with a hint of impatience, and reached into her shoulder-bag for her cigarettes. 'You don't mind if I smoke?' Without waiting for a reply, she lit one and exhaled smoke towards the sky. 'I've known Patrick for a long time,' she went on smoothly, 'and all I'm saying is, don't make any more of a fool of yourself than you already have! You're a damned good assistant, and I don't want to lose you. You can't be blamed for catching the flu, after all...'

In spite of her tension, Gabriella hid a smile at her boss's sweeping generosity.

'...and I suppose the cyclone was unavoidable...'

'Yes, fairly unavoidable.' Gabriella's faint attempt at levity fell on unappreciative ears. Ursula levelled a cold blue gaze on her.

'...but Patrick's a hardened cynic, my dear. And you're so young and gullible.'

Not any more, Gabriella wanted to say. Not
since Piers. And definitely not since her spell on
the Ile des Couleuvres with Rick...

'He's thirty-four, far too old for you,' Ursula
was continuing calmly, 'and of course he's absolutely no intention of settling down and tying
himself to one woman. Heavens, I should know!'

'Are you...?' Gabriella could hardly bring
herself to frame the question. She swallowed
convulsively, felt as if she was sinking, sub-
merging in the pain of this encounter. 'Are you
in love with him?'

'I've been in love with him for years,' Ursula
said flatly. 'But much good it's done me!'

But you're married, Gabriella said silently, her
hands clenching into small fists at her sides. And
Rick knows you're married...

For some reason, in spite of all the evidence,
she found it difficult to believe that the Rick
Josephs she'd begun to get to know this last
couple of days was capable of carrying on an
adulterous affair over a long period of time.
Perhaps she *was* hopelessly naïve, just as Rick
said, just as Ursula said. Speechless, she waited
for Ursula's next move.

'Look, my dear, all I'm saying is that, pro-
viding there's no repeat performance, I'm prepared to overlook what's happened so far,' the
dark woman said with a tight smile. 'There's an
enormous amount of work to be done to organise this shoot, as we both know. Oh, and

there's a party tonight, in honour of everyone's eventual arrival! Formal dress, down in the poolside restaurant and gardens. There's going to be a *séga* show, with audience participation, if any of us have got the strength to participate after this wretched flu. So, I suggest you get dressed and come over to my suite and we'll discuss these locations...'

'*Séga*?' To her chagrin, she was feeling overpowered by the other woman's forcefulness. Ursula hadn't reached fashion editor status with *First Flair* without a daunting capacity for steamrollering the opposition. Gabriella felt as if she'd been appropriately dressed-down, court-martialled and pardoned, all in the space of about five minutes...

'*Séga* is the local African-based dance,' Ursula supplied briefly. 'Very colourful and provocative. We might use some shots of it in the feature. So, are we all sorted out, Gabriella? Let's get on with it, shall we? And leave Patrick St Josef to his own devices?'

'He...' Gabriella cleared a husky throat. 'He's not the photographer for the shoot, then?'

'He should have been,' Ursula said grimly, stubbing out her cigarette on the tiled balcony with the high heel of her tan sandal. 'In fact I was rather proud of my little *coup* in persuading him. Normally he's far too much of a high-flyer to do run-of-the-mill magazine fashion shoots.

But after our little . . . disagreement . . . he walked out on me!'

'I see. What did you . . . disagree over?' She couldn't help herself, she had to ask.

Ursula had stood up, preparing to leave. The look she slanted at Gabriella as she strolled towards the door was curiously hard and speculative.

'My dear girl, you mean in all your cosy intimacy, marooned on your little island, he didn't tell you?' Ursula lifted an ironic eyebrow at Gabriella's tense face. 'My husband cited Patrick in his petition for divorce.' She smiled thinly. 'And Patrick being Patrick, shunning any kind of long-term commitment to *anyone*, didn't like that one little bit!'

CHAPTER EIGHT

AT LEAST she had a glamorous, exotic setting to feel absolutely suicidal in, Gabriella reflected, gazing at the party in full swing around her. And at least she was more appropriately dressed than for her first evening here...

Crowds of chattering, laughing, vividly dressed people thronged the lush, subtropical gardens. The hotel's kidney-shaped swimming-pool was surrounded by white-clothed tables. Each bore glass-domed yellow candles, flickering like scores of glow-worms in the darkness. Above these, floodlights bathed the whole area in a romantic golden glow, turning the palm-tree fronds to an unnaturally brilliant emerald-green, and the water in the pool to a deep, mysterious jade.

She thought of that first evening, when she'd seen Rick with the sophisticated group at the bar. Tonight was just the same, only more so...

That should have been the clue to his identity, she realised grimly. Seeing him in the company of gorgeous women who could only be models. Seeing the way they'd fawned over him, the way they'd seemed to be making him the centre of attention. She should have suspected straight away that he was someone important, or famous, or both...

Although with his looks and personality he'd probably receive widespread female adulation even if he were a dustman, she acknowledged bitterly.

She shivered, in spite of the warm humidity of the evening. Rick *was* Ursula's lover. Now there was no further room for doubt, she could see what a gullible idiot she'd been, Gabriella thought, swallowing on a hard lump in her throat as she smiled and waved at another familiar face from a famous modelling agency. She should have known. All the incriminating evidence had been there. She'd had her suspicions right from the start. She'd just shelved them, as she'd begun to fall under the spell of Rick's personality. The more deeply attractive she'd found him, the harder it had been to believe he was capable of such perfidy. She hadn't *wanted* to believe it...

The decibels of the party were increasing. An African band with an electric guitar and wide tambourine-style drums had begun to play rhythmical, jaunty music, reminiscent of Latin-American. The models, in attempts to upstage each other, were appearing in ever more outrageous outfits. *First Flair*'s fashion department were clearly vying for attention as well.

Exchanging cheerful greetings with colleagues and a few of the models she knew, she privately prayed that an appropriately festive outer packaging would conceal her bleak inner despair. The only dress she'd brought with her for formal parties on this trip was in a shimmery gold, with a fitted, strapless satin bodice, and a full, ballerina-length taffeta skirt. With her normally pale olive skin warmed by the beginnings of a light golden tan, the sparkly material looked a lot better on her than it had when she'd tried it on in the January sales. With strappy gold sandals and pearl choker and earrings, she hoped the effect was suitably sophisticated and that it dazzled the eye sufficiently to hide her misery.

Sarah, a plump, pretty, auburn-haired make-up girl from the fashion department, was waving and smiling from a table by the pool, and Gabriella changed course, weaving a path towards her.

'Gaby! Come and sit here and tell *all*! Is it *true*?'

She'd barely sat down at the table to join her friend, and stiffened in disbelief at the pert question.

'Is what true?'

'There's a rumour flying round that Ursula went searching for you, and found you and Patrick St Josef *in flagrante*, Gaby! What *have* you been up to, you dark little horse?'

White-faced, Gabriella managed a tight smile. 'Wouldn't you like to know!' she fenced lightly. 'But do bear in mind that rumours get embroidered as they go round, Sarah!'

Sarah was scrutinising her with wry concern. 'Maybe. Well, whatever you've been up to, love, it hasn't done you much good! You look stressed-out.'

'I happen to be recovering from a bout of flu!' Gabriella protested, with a short laugh. 'And there's nothing very romantic about that!'

Privately, she was dismayed at her friend's damning verdict on her appearance. She'd washed and blow-dried her blonde hair, and left it in a shiny mane down her back. She'd been hoping that the soft green eye-shadow, tawny-pink blusher and russet-pink lipstick hid the tension in her face. In short, she thought ruefully, she'd made the best she could of a bad job. And after a gruelling afternoon with Ursula, going over her notes and suggestions, and drawing up a detailed itinerary for the following day, and since Ursula had spelled out, in so many words, the truth about her relationship with Patrick St Josef, she'd needed to...

'Well, in my experience there's no smoke without fire, so don't be boring and disappoint me!' Sarah laughed, smoothing the skirt of her emerald chiffon dress and crossing shapely legs. 'And besides, I've seen pictures of Patrick St Josef in one of those glossy magazine articles about him, and wow!' Sarah moaned in mock-desire. 'Gaby, he is one *hunky* male! I'd be caught *in flagrante* with him any day!'

Sarah was so comical that Gabriella couldn't help it, she had to laugh. She found herself joining her friend in helpless mirth. But inside she was aching. And seething with frustration and embarrassment. How come *she* hadn't recognised Rick from some magazine article? Why had she been so ignorant and easily fooled? How he must have been laughing behind her back at her stupidity...!

'The food smells mouthwatering,' Sarah was enthusing, eyes shining. 'Have you seen the buffet table? Fish creole, tandoori chicken, braised venison...'

'I'm not terribly hungry,' Gabriella had to confess, feeling like the ultimate party-killer. 'I think it's an after-effect of the flu...'

It was a lonely experience, she decided, feeling bleakly tense when everyone around her was talking and laughing and mingling and sipping cocktails, electrified with excitement and anticipation. The velvety warm night smelled exotic, heady with the scent of tropical flowers. The star-speckled southern sky, impossibly dark blue behind the floodlights, the pulsing *séga* music, the glamorously dressed models and chicly elegant *First Flair* staff...everything seemed to be combining to make her feel like the spectre at the feast.

She was so taut with nerves that she jumped violently when a familiar deep, gravelly voice behind them said, 'Can I offer you iced champagne, ladies?'

She spun round in her chair, and her heart plummeted wildly in her chest. Rick stood there, darkly sardonic, holding a silver tray bearing a bottle of champagne in a silver ice bucket, and two glasses.

Sarah blinked at him, clearly startled.

'Oh—er—champagne?' she began doubtfully, staring at him more closely. 'We didn't order——'

'Rick, what are you doing here?' Gabriella cut in quietly, every pulse in her body drumming in apprehension. Champagne on ice? Couldn't he let her forget the silly challenge she'd thrown at him that first night?

'Posing as a waiter?' he suggested calmly, pulling out a chair and sitting down on the other side of Sarah. Lifting a hand, he somehow managed to summon the head waiter out of thin air. 'Bring another glass, would you, René?'

'*Bien sûr*, Monsieur St Josef...' The waiter scurried away and Sarah turned wide eyes on Rick, comprehension dawning. Pink-cheeked, she stuttered,

'You're Patrick St Josef! Of course, I recognise you now!' She laughed, going even pinker, with a nervous glance at Gabriella, adding in a mock-puzzled undertone, 'Why is he joking about posing as a waiter?'

'Because he's gatecrashing?' Gabriella suggested tightly, eyeing Rick with deep indignation. 'I got the impression from Ursula,' she told him, hating him for his nonchalant amusement as he leaned back in his chair and levelled a cool gaze at her, 'that she's furious you left her in the lurch over this fashion shoot, and that you weren't invited to this party!'

'*Tant pis*.' He shrugged dismissively, a wickedly taunting glint in his eyes. 'No matter. I am staying here. Can the hotel exclude troublesome guests from joining in these festivities, if they so wish? Sadly, I fear not. Aren't you going to introduce me to your friend, Gaby?'

His cool, teasing unconcern was infuriating. Rigid with combined anger and self-consciousness, she gritted her teeth.

'Troublesome guests are supposed to be confined to that roped-off section over there,' she pointed out with acid politeness. 'This is an invitation-only, pre-shoot party, and if Ursula sees you I can probably kiss my job goodbye...'

She scanned the colourful, crowded party scene beyond their table, expecting Ursula to descend on them any moment like Nemesis, goddess of vengeance. 'However, this is Sarah Clarke, one of the make-up specialists from *First Flair*. Sarah, this, as you've already gathered, is Patrick St Josef.'

'I'm thrilled to meet you.' Sarah, with an incredulous reaction to Gabriella's rudeness, held out her hand. Gabriella watched as Rick shook it solemnly. 'I've been an admirer of your work for ages,' Sarah cooed, blossoming visibly under that glinting amber scrutiny. 'I *loved* that cover portrait you did recently!'

Sarah gushed on. Rick murmured polite words of response. The extra glass arrived and the head waiter deferentially poured three measures of champagne. All the while, Gabriella found her eyes glued, against her will, on Rick. She felt as if her heart was in her mouth. Every atom in her body seemed to be quivering with response to his nearness, quite irrespective of the stern mental messages her brain was issuing on the subject . . .

He was dark and devastating in tropical white dinner-jacket, dark trousers, discreet olive silk bow-tie. Everything about him now seemed tauntingly familiar, after the intimacy they'd shared. And yet at the same time he seemed a stranger to her.

In the flickering candlelight, his eyes gleamed antique gold. His straight dark hair flopped in its habitual thick forelock over his eyebrows. The hard, bony jaw already bore the faint traces of bluish-black shadow. When he smiled, his teeth were dazzlingly white in contrast. As she watched him talking to Sarah, listening, gravely attentive, exerting that effortless charm, he looked so heart-stoppingly attractive that all Gabriella's firm resolutions were in danger of sinking without trace.

She wanted to reach out her hand and touch him. She felt hot all over.

'Excuse me,' she said tautly, pushing her champagne away and standing up abruptly, 'there's someone over there I need to talk to...'

Blindly pushing between the tables, she fixed her eyes on a path which led between an arch of royal palms and a clump of casuarinas, and plunged down it. It led towards the beach. By the time she'd kicked off her gold shoes, felt the caster-sugar sand tickling her toes, she realised she was choking back tears. She blinked them away, fiercely, walking with angry, rapid strides down to the edge of the lagoon.

The sheltered calm of the water hemmed in by the reef reflected the moon. Silver coins of light dotted the surface. In a purple-black sky, the moon itself hung like a massive white balloon.

Suddenly weak at the knees, she sank to the sand, and hugged her arms round herself. Rick's appearance at her side, looming out of the moonlit darkness, made her stomach sink despairingly.

'Please go away,' she said quietly, dashing the back of one hand over her eyes, uncaring of the green eyeshadow. 'I don't want to talk to you...'

'But I need to talk to you,' he countered calmly, sitting down beside her, a considerate space away, and turning his head to search her face thoughtfully.

'No, you don't,' she informed him bitterly. 'You had endless opportunities to *talk* to me while we were marooned on your island. You just want to make a few excuses, make yourself feel better. Forget it! It doesn't matter, I told you...'

'Gaby...' The deep voice was cool, with that teasing mockery ever present. 'You've spent a lot of time telling me how mature you are. Don't try to tell me that what happened on my island doesn't matter. We both know it matters...'

Twisting stiffly to face him, she clenched her fists at her sides.

'All right. So what? I made a fool of myself... I imagined something... something deeply *romantic* was taking place! Then I found it wasn't! I'll survive! As you keep telling me, I'm *very* young and naïve!'

'Gabriella...' He reached to take her hand, his fingers closing tightly round hers as she tensed to pull away. '*Ecoute-moi*, Gaby. I can see how you might feel... betrayed, because I didn't reveal my real identity.'

'Can you?' She trembled as he turned her palm over in his hand, smoothed the soft swell of her thumb joint with a rhythmical motion. Fiercely defensive, she snatched her hand violently away. 'Why, Rick? Why did you have to be so... sneaky? Why didn't you tell me who you were?'

He was silent for a few moments. Raking both hands abruptly through his hair, he gave a soft, self-mocking groan.

'If I tell you the reason, it sounds conceited!' he admitted in a low, husky voice. He slanted a faint grin at her. 'Hell, I'm not that famous! It's only normally within the fashion world that I'm subjected to the...sycophantic treatment. But even so, it happens often enough to become tiresome. When I barged into Ursula's room, and met her beautiful blonde assistant, and she appeared not to know me from Adam, it was like...a breath of fresh air. Can you understand that?'

'No, I can't! When you say it felt like "a breath of fresh air", what you're really saying is you saw a chance for some amusement! An inexperienced pushover to make a fool of...'

'*Dieu*, Gaby! Where is your self-esteem?' he grated impatiently, twisting to inspect her white face more closely. 'How can an intelligent, talented, beautiful young woman put herself down so much?'

'I do have self-esteem,' she countered shakily, stiffening at the accusation. 'And...if I'm honest, I don't regret what happened between us on your island, Rick. I knew what I wanted...' She gave a short, painful laugh. 'For the first time in my life, I—I knew how I felt...'

'Gaby...' His voice was hoarser, the wry humour deepening to husky emotion.

'I just didn't understand the situation, that's all. And that's your fault, for not *telling* me!'

'The situation?' he queried quietly.

'The   truth...about   who   you   were and——'

'In what way would telling you my real name have changed anything?' he cut in calmly. 'I did not lie to you. I often use the name Rick Josephs. It's only an abbreviation of my full name. And if you want to know why I didn't reveal my professional identity, it was because there was something about you...something that made me want, very badly, to get to know you on an equal basis. Without the complication of...preconceived ideas.'

'How insulting,' she said flatly, 'to imply that if I'd recognised you I'd have behaved any differently with you!'

'Wouldn't you?' His expression was ironic. 'Let me give you an example, Gaby. You saw the way your friend Sarah reacted, when she knew who I was. Multiply that reaction a dozen times, and that's the way most new introductions go. There are times when I wonder if anyone is interested in *me*, the real person I am...'

She glanced at him, hiding her surprise, a faint *frisson* of empathy touching her frozen emotions. She suppressed it quickly.

'Now who's lacking in self-esteem?' she taunted lightly. 'And you honestly expect me to believe that load of...*garbage*?'

He shrugged, bestowing one of his deprecating grins on her which undermined her steeled defences to an alarming degree. She caught her breath, fighting her own weakness.

'Perhaps that is expecting too much,' he agreed drily, 'from a defensive little soul such as yours, Gabriella.'

'Besides,' she persisted scornfully, 'never mind your real name, and your... your so-called angst at being famous. Right from the start, you stayed cleverly ambiguous on the subject of Ursula. Made me feel bad about jumping to conclusions! And all the time you *were* her lover!'

Her voice broke a fraction on the last few words. Furious with herself, she caught her hand to her mouth, pressing her knuckles against her lips. She was trembling all over with pent-up misery.

'I was?' The deep voice was flat, but a note of cool steel had crept in. 'Perhaps you'd like to reveal the source of your information on that, Gaby.'

'Oh, stop it!' She couldn't take any more of this subtle fencing. 'Stop it! Who do you think told me? Ursula herself, of course! But she didn't really need to, did she? It was obvious, right from the start, if only I hadn't let myself be... be *dazzled* by your charm!'

There was a silence after this outburst. It lengthened into a tense, endless blackness between them.

'So *that* is what happened?' Rick's voice was heavily ironic when he spoke at last. 'You were dazzled by my charm?'

'That's the only excuse I can come up with,' she agreed with bitter humour. 'So never worry your handsome head about your public persona being your only attraction. You have plenty of charisma as just plain Rick Josephs...'

'I'm deeply indebted to you for the re-assurance. But you know something, Gabriella? I find myself developing a degree of sympathy for Piers Wellington.'

The cool statement was unbearably provocative. She stared at him incredulously.

'Really?' she bit out. 'Because you know how it feels to be found out?'

'No, *ma petite*. Because I'm beginning to wonder if he was subjected to this same blinkered trial without jury.'

She couldn't believe her ears. A wave of heat washed over her, followed by a sick ache in the pit of her stomach. She should never have risked confiding in him. She'd been *mad* to tell him about Piers. She should have known he was not to be trusted with something as private and personal as the trauma with Piers...

'That's just about the lowest line of attack you could have chosen!' Unsteadily, she began to climb to her feet. 'I must need my head examining for getting involved with you...'

'So fickle,' he murmured implacably, un-coiling athletically from the sand and blocking her escape. 'And I could say ditto, Gabriella . . .'

'You're not involved with anyone but yourself!'

'Untrue.' He encircled her upper arms with his fingers, effectively imprisoning her on the spot. 'And you have a lamentably vicious tongue when you're upset . . .'

She was taut as a bowstring when he dropped his dark head to kiss her. When the firm coolness of his lips covered hers, she resisted as long as she was physically able, and then with a choking shudder she found herself parting her mouth, al-lowing his tongue intimate access without the strength to fight.

'You can't deny this, Gaby . . .' he breathed against her mouth. 'There may not be trust, _chérie_, but there is a fire between us . . .'

'No . . .' It wasn't a convincing denial. She was shivering uncontrollably as he pulled her possessively against the hard warmth of his chest, crushing her convulsively to him with a strong, sweeping caress which brought her into dis-turbing contact with the entire length of his body. Every inch of her responded traitorously to the sensation of the long, steel-muscled body over-poweringly close to hers.

'No?' he taunted harshly, drawing back a fraction to inspect her hectic cheeks in the moon-light. 'Gabriella, there is something I want you to know...'

'Hey there! Patrick——?' It was a seductive female voice, hailing him from the top of the beach. 'Patrick?'

The tension simmered between them as they broke slowly apart. Catching her lower lip between her teeth, Gabriella turned to see who was coming across the beach.

'The *séga* show is starting, Patrick, darling!'

Gabriella recognised her. It was one of the svelte, impossibly long-limbed and glamorous models she'd seen fawning over Rick that first evening, at the bar. She was swaying over the sand towards them, with a loping cat-walk slink, like the legendary 'Girl from Ipanema'. 'We want you to come and dance with us!'

'Then you're going to be disappointed.' Rick's wry, drawling response was enough to convey cold anger at the interruption. The girl tossed back her waist-length black hair, and flashed a wide, unrepentant smile from Rick to Gabriella.

'Oh, sorry,' she said with blatant insincerity. 'Was I interrupting something?'

'Yes.' Rick bestowed a ruthlessly mocking smile on the girl. 'In fact——'

'No! You're not,' Gabriella cut in hastily, guessing that he was about to issue an even more scathing put-down to the girl. 'Why don't you go and dance with them, Rick?'

Rick's face was shadowed against the moon-light, but his cool fury was almost tangible.

'Gaby...' The deep voice held a warning command.

Twisting decisively out of his treacherous embrace, she bent quickly to retrieve her sandals from the sand,

'Go ahead,' she urged sweetly, smiling calmly at the girl. 'I'd just about had enough in any case!'

'But you must come too, Gabriella,' Rick said, ruthlessly polite, catching hold of her arm in a punishing grip as she would have pushed past him and made her escape. 'You'd enjoy *séga*. It comes from the African and Malagasy slaves shipped over here in the seventeenth century. At the same time as those imported French wives, remember?'

'I seem to have a vague recollection of the story,' she conceded tensely, wincing in his grip as they began to walk back up the beach.

'*Séga* is a courtship drama,' he went on implacably. They'd reached the lush flowering trees in the hotel gardens and the sensual drumming rhythm from the dance-floor could be heard more clearly. 'But it is the female who taunts and provokes and tantalises the male...'

'I'm *really* not interested.'

'No? I'd have thought it was very much in your line, Gaby.' He retained the grip on her arm, imprisoning her at his side. 'It starts slowly. The beat intensifies. They move closer, they sway and undulate, but they never touch. At the command *en bas*, the woman sinks to her knees, bends backwards, like a limbo dancer. The man extends his body over hers, but still they do not touch... it is a parody of sexual surrender...'

'*Rick*...please!' It was a hoarse, angry whisper as she was propelled along.

The dark-haired model was listening to Rick's husky, cruelly mocking tone of voice, casting uncertain and rather jealous glances at Gabriella. Mortified and pink-cheeked, Gabriella stared fixedly ahead of her.

They'd reached the edge of the dance-floor. The drums and the music were pulsating and insistent. The dancers were in mid-performance, their skin gleaming a rich mahogany, the man in skin-tight yellow breeches and a colourful shirt, the woman bare-midriffed, in a hip-clinging red-flowered skirt billowing out into fullness. Mesmerised, conscious of Rick's closeness behind her, Gabriella watched the age-old ritual of love and desire, enacted in mime.

It was provocative and exciting and beautifully done, but in her present state of mind she could hardly bear to watch it.

'Does it make the blood flow warmer in your defensive little heart, Gabriella?' he murmured in her ear, folding strongly possessive arms around her and crushing her backwards against him, his breath warm on her neck. 'Does it remind you of the touching way you revealed your desire for me on the island?'

She stiffened in shocked disbelief. He was hateful, insufferable . . . ! Trembling inside, her pulses jumping wildly, she writhed to get away. Rick's grasp on her tightened. Catching her breath angrily in her throat, she whirled round on him, pushing fiercely but unsuccessfully at his chest, uncaring of interested spectators near by who were turning to watch her struggles.

'What's wrong, Gaby?' he taunted in a low voice. 'You haven't suddenly become prim and prudish again, have you? That night we spent together was a revelation, *mignonne*. Don't disillusion me again . . .'

'The dancing is beautiful, but you're . . . despicable!' she ground out unevenly, heat coursing through her as she wrestled against his hard embrace. 'I wish I'd never met you!'

'But you said you loved me, Gabriella,' he pointed out, huskily ruthless. 'And you made it very hard for me to walk away from you. Did it mean nothing? Giving yourself to me? Letting me be the first to make love to you?'

'Rick, *please* . . . !' She was breathless with shame, conscious of eyes swivelling in covert fascination. 'Stop this . . .' Her voice was strangled in her throat.

'Not until I get an answer,' he murmured grimly. 'Why did you tell me you loved me, Gaby, if you weren't prepared to trust me? Or did you get love confused with desire? A brief rush of hormones, as short-lived as a high fever?'

'What do you *want* from me?' she sobbed, oblivious to everything but this stormy vacuum of tension between Rick and herself. The dance had reached its hot, shimmering crescendo, the drumbeat gathering speed and volume so that it seemed to echo the hectic thud of her own heartbeat as the blood raced to the surface of her skin. A sudden burst of applause heralded the finale. 'I told you how I felt! I was honest with you! Do you expect me to grovel at your feet now that I've discovered you were lying to me all the time?'

'What you feel for me,' he told her with soft emphasis, 'what I feel for you…it's new and raw and neither of us has had time to reflect on it, Gaby. We need time to explore our feelings. We need some trust…'

'*Trust*? I trusted you and then you made a mockery of that trust,' she retorted, in a low, intense voice. 'Now I don't know how I feel. I'm confused, and I'm angry…'

'And *I* can scarcely believe my *eyes*,' Ursula's voice purred maliciously behind them. Rick didn't loosen his hold on her, but Gabriella went very still as she turned to meet the furious blue glare of her boss.

'I warned you, Gabriella. It seems to me it might be wise if you began to look for another job as soon as you get back to London, my dear.'

With a choked sob, Gabriella wrenched free from Rick's grasp, and stood trembling all over with fury and indignation. The older woman, designer-elegant in clinging geometric black and white silk, surveyed Gabriella's slender figure in the gold dress, a gleam of acute dislike in the ice-blue eyes.

'Don't worry,' Gabriella heard herself retort unsteadily, choking back tears. 'You can have my resignation, as of now...!'

'*Merde*, Ursula!' Rick's harshly authoritative voice grated with cold anger. 'Don't you think you've done enough harm already? Do you get a kick out of being such a complete *bitch*?'

Ursula's face paled at the caustic insult. 'How dare you——?' she began frigidly.

'No, how dare you?' he drawled with hard distaste. 'And I warn you, interfere in my personal life any further and I can't vouch for the permanence of your own job!'

'You might be a famous photographer, Patrick, but give me one valid reason why you imagine you could wield sufficient influence to affect my job!'

'Being the new owner of *First Flair* magazine, among others.'

The cool retort seemed to hang in the warm night air between them. Rick's dark face was a mask, utterly expressionless. But there was an implacable glint in his eyes.

'What...?' Ursula's face lost its haughty composure. Blue eyes widening, she was staring at Rick as if he'd just flown in from another planet. 'Are you serious? *You're* the new owner of the magazine?'

There was an interested circle of listeners by now: Sarah, and the dark-haired model, and half a dozen others standing near by and agog to pick up on scandal or gossip being played out under their very noses...

Their faces were just a pale blur to Gabriella. Her knees feeling even more ill-equipped to support her, she switched a white-faced gaze from Ursula to Rick, slowly shaking her head.

'Right this moment, Rick, I really couldn't care if you've just bought every glossy magazine from London to New York.' Her voice was husky with tears, but tightly controlled. 'I'm just not interested. So if you'll excuse me, you two can carry on playing your cheap little power games. I'm catching the next plane back to England...'

CHAPTER NINE

IN THE bustle of Plaisance Airport in the morning, Gabriella stood in a queue for the check-in, gazing unseeingly past the other passengers, longing for the flight to be on time. It was quite ridiculous, but until she was safely on board that red and white Air Mauritius jet, emblazoned with its native bird emblem, she felt as twitchy as a wanted criminal.

Her dash to pack and escape last night had been hampered by the fear that at any moment Ursula might appear to berate her, or command her to fulfil her obligations—worse still, that Rick might try to stop her. But in fact her hurried retreat had passed off without incident. Checking out of the hotel had also gone off smoothly. Neither Rick nor Ursula was to be seen. Most likely they were tearing each other limb from limb at some prearranged venue, and good luck to them; they deserved each other, she thought acidly.

The fact that he hadn't even cared enough to come and say goodbye wasn't in the least surprising, she told herself firmly. Didn't it just go to prove how unimportant she was, in the grand scheme of his life? The sooner she put several thousand miles between them, the better her wounded pride would feel...

And the happier Rick would be, she felt bitterly certain, relieved of any false obligations to apologise, or explain, or justify...

He felt guilty for deceiving her. He was cursing his weakness for giving in to her that night on the Ile des Couleuvres. There was a degree of proud possessiveness, maybe. The typically male preference for keeping control of a relationship, of being the one to end it, and not the other way around. He hadn't liked her walking out on him, when he'd ordered her to stay...

But guilt and pity were the overriding factors in his feelings towards her. What was complicating the whole thing, Gabriella felt sure, was the fact that she'd blurted out her secret feelings, told him she loved him. Now he was feeling sorry for her...

She couldn't bear to think of him *pitying* her. That was the worst thing of all.

As for his cool confrontation with Ursula, his revelation that he'd bought the magazine...her head was too dizzy with her own emotions to take it in. Rick Josephs...Patrick St Josef...now owned *First Flair*? Was it possible? The ownership of the magazine had been rumoured to be about to change hands, she knew that. And very rich people like Patrick St Josef were quite capable of buying it. Presumably Rick was telling the truth, although, a cynical little voice reminded her, one couldn't be one hundred per cent sure about that. First, he'd kept her in the dark about his real name. Then about his true involvement with Ursula Taylor. And then about his surprise back-door take-over of *First Flair* ...

She seethed when she recalled their conversation, that night at the *campement*; how he'd kept a deadpan expression when she'd talked about the possibility of the Wellington Group buying the magazine, voiced her fears over her own job because of Piers's malice ...

And all the time he'd known he was buying it himself ...

He'd shown a marked talent for deception. In all, she deduced militantly, he was about as dependable as a man-eating shark in a swimming-pool ...

She'd had a twinge of guilt about *First Flair* footing her bill, but on reflection she'd earned it. She'd worked very hard on their behalf since arriving in Mauritius. She hadn't even had time to swim in that sapphire-blue sea ...

Having checked with the receptionist about the time of the next flight back to London, she'd called a taxi and driven down the coast to another hotel, nearer the airport, for the night. Slightly ashamed of herself for such cowardly escape tactics, she'd quickly calmed her conscience. There was no way she could have faced Ursula again last night. As for Rick ...

She shuddered involuntarily, clenching her fingers around the handle of her suitcase. In a short sage-green silk culotte suit, flat tan sandals, her hair in a high French plait, dark glasses firmly in position to hide her puffy red eyes, composure felt fragile but sustainable. But images of their brief time together kept flicking relentlessly through her head, like a silent slide-show. Her unhappiness felt like a ball of lead in her chest, pressing in on her until she couldn't breathe...

If she never had to see him again for the rest of her life, she'd still wince with humiliation whenever she thought about him. With an involuntary glow of shame burning her cheeks, she remembered how she'd felt, when she'd wanted him to make love to her, how surprised she'd been at the emotional intensity of her desire. Fierce, and deep-flowing, and completely new, like nothing she'd experienced before. The things he'd murmured to her, the intimate things she'd said to him, so unavoidable in the heat of the night, uninhibited and shocking when recalled in the cruel light of reality...

Cringing silently in self-derision, she squeezed her eyes shut in an agony of remorse and despair and prayed for amnesia to obliterate the pain...

When there was a polite tap on her shoulder, she jumped violently, her eyes flying open apprehensively. Two airport officials stood there, smiling. In neat uniforms, they looked gravely polite and courteous, but she stared at them as if they were holding guns at her head.

'Yes ... ? Is something wrong?'

'Mademoiselle Howard? Gabriella Howard?' They were calmly non-committal. 'May we see your passport, please?'

Slowly, her mind reeling, she dug in her shoulder-bag and produced it.

'Is there a problem?' she persisted, an edge in her voice.

'No problem, *mademoiselle* ...' One of the officials, a kindly-looking Indian with warm brown eyes, scanned the passport, gave a satisfied nod and slipped it into his pocket. 'But there is an urgent message for you. So please come with us.'

Protests overruled, she found herself escorted firmly out of the airport terminal. Wildly, she reviewed the possibilities. False arrest? Mistaken identity? Did they think she was a drug smuggler? A terrorist in disguise? Mauritius was a peaceful, friendly little island, but she'd heard they treated law-breaking very seriously, that they had quite rigid export laws ... did they think she was trying to take forbidden items out of the country?

Or was this maybe some kind of warped revenge of Ursula's? Her method of retaliation when dogsbody assistants had the nerve to walk out on her in the middle of a fashion shoot ...

'I'm sure there's been some mistake,' she began. 'And before I go anywhere with you, I'd like to see your identification, please.'

Both men stopped, and calmly produced small ID wallets, verifying their status as airport security officials. Struggling for calm, she was half expecting to be frog-marched to a police car, but instead they appeared to be steering her towards a bright yellow helicopter, waiting on the tarmac.

'Just a minute,' she began, suspicion beginning to mount. 'What's going on? What exactly is this urgent message...?'

'Have no fear, *mademoiselle*. There is a person who wishes to speak with you...'

Rick, relaxed as a beach bum in sawn-off denims and white T-shirt, wearing black headphones and mouthpiece, was calmly sitting in the pilot's seat. A smile of grim satisfaction tilted the corners of his mouth when he saw her.

Digging in her heels, Gabriella brought her escorts to an abrupt halt.

'Oh, no...!' she began breathlessly, fury tingling through her. Swivelling to the man with the brown eyes, she said reasonably, 'No! This person may wish to speak with me, but *I* do not wish to speak with this person, do you understand?'

The kindly man smiled, and propelled her a few feet closer to the helicopter. Rick had jumped down, and was strolling over to them. She'd never noticed what a subtle swagger he had when he walked, she decided angrily. A loping, loose-limbed, supremely masculine walk, the kind which drew female eyes like a magnet...

'How could you have me *dragged* from the airport?' she began, so furious that her voice cracked in mid-sentence. 'Who do you think you are? The ... the chief of police or something?'

'No,' he grinned, taking her arm and hauling her towards the passenger seat. 'But the chief of police is an old friend of mine. Gaby, stop making a scene and come quietly...'

'No, I won't!' She kicked and fought like a wildcat. 'This *is* a democratic island, isn't it? I'm not going anywhere with you. I want my passport back, *now*! And I want to get on that plane to London ... !'

'If you still want to fly back to London tomorrow, I will personally deliver you to the airport,' he told her gravely, accepting her passport from one of her unrepentant escorts. 'For now, *ma petite*, you are coming with me. Ouch!' he spat, his dark eyebrows knitting in grim amusement as one of her kicks made vicious contact with his shin. 'Stop fighting me, you little hoyden! Calm down, and do as you're damn well told!'

'I will *not* ...'

Without warning, he lifted her bodily into the passenger seat of the helicopter, tossed her suitcase on to the rear seats, and slammed the door decisively after her.

Toying with the idea of leaping straight out again, she caught sight of the humorous exchange of glances between the two officials, as they shrugged and exchanged joking words with Rick, and she was suddenly too overcome with fury and indignation to move.

All right, she told herself, breathing deeply to calm herself. She wouldn't give them all the amusement and satisfaction of watching her resist. Retreating into outraged disdain seemed the best option.

What kind of despot was he, to connive with his friends, arrange for her to be intercepted, plan to abduct her in a helicopter, dominate her in this despicable fashion? Waves of anger coursed through her. When he finally came around the helicopter, calmly checked the rotors, and climbed in beside her, she was shivering with rage.

He handed her a set of headphones.

'I don't want them, thanks,' she told him icily. 'I shan't want to talk to you anyway.'

'It's a noisy ride without them,' he pointed out mildly. 'Wear them, Gaby.'

After a mutinous silence, she snatched them from him and slammed them on to her head, folding her arms and staring rigidly in front of her.

'I could probably have you prosecuted over this,' she informed him coldly. 'I'm sure it's against the law, forcing people to get into helicopters against their will! The nasty little word *kidnapping* springs to mind, in fact...'

'Quite likely. Still, remember my ancestry, Gabriella.' His voice held a rough edge of humour as he pressed the starter button, and the rotors overhead began to turn. 'For a man descended from pirates, and wife-importers, kidnapping is tame behaviour.'

After a brief relay of information to the control tower, the helicopter lifted abruptly into the air, whirled tightly to the north, and rose into the brilliant sunlight.

The trip up the coast of Mauritius was accomplished in silence. Gabriella, gazing down at the weird mountain peaks and dramatic changes in landscape, could hardly believe it when they dropped down to land on a deserted white beach, and she realised, as the dust and sand settled around them, that Rick had brought her back to the Ile des Couleuvres.

'Here we are.' He flipped off his headphones and jumped down from the helicopter. 'Welcome back to my island, Gabriella.'

'Don't be such a *hypocrite* . . . !' she snapped, stiffening as he grabbed her hand and tugged her down from her seat. 'And how you can behave like this, when you're mixed up in Ursula Taylor's divorce, I just can't——'

'*Tais toi,*' he murmured hoarsely, catching her in his arms and hauling her against him. He flipped off her sunglasses, scanning her angry face with grim humour. 'Shut up, Gaby, and let me talk to you, sweetheart . . .'

'I'm *not* your sweetheart . . .'

She was wrestling furiously with him, and they both fell to the sand. The fine powder-softness of the surface was warmed by the sun, and as Rick restrained her furious struggles and they rolled in fierce embrace it subsided sensuously beneath her, in silent connivance.

'Gaby, darling Gaby...' A persuasive catch of emotion in the deep murmur touched a buried chord in her, in spite of her blind fury.

With a choked sob, she found her mouth covered by Rick's firm, seeking lips. And the present injustices of her situation temporarily melted into oblivion as the emotional hunger flickered into life all over again.

'Rick, this isn't fair...' she whispered huskily, as he smoothed long, devouring caresses over her writhing body, his hands moulding the tender swell of her breasts through the sage-green silk. 'I don't know what it is you want from me, but——'

'Everything...' he breathed wryly, kissing her lips, her throat, raking impatient hands into her blonde plait and teasing it free from its restraints. 'I want everything from you, *chérie*, and then a little more. Whatever it is you've managed to do to me, Gaby, I'm an emotional wreck without you...'

She stared up into the narrowed gleam of his eyes, saw the ironic twist of his mouth, and trembled at the force of her own feelings.

'Don't expect any sympathy from *me*!' she said unsteadily. 'You're just a convincing fraud! You're a confidence artist, Patrick St Josef! You just don't like being thwarted, do you? You don't want me, you just want me to do things *your* way...'

'If you insist, that can be arranged.' It was a soft growl of impatience against her hair. 'I was planning on talking first, but if the only way to reason with you is like this I'm happy to oblige...'

With the audacity of one of his buccaneering forebears, he slid questing fingers along the buttons of her blouse, succeeding in unfastening them with a speed which left her reeling. The touch of his fingers on the sensitive swell of her breasts was sheer torture. She gasped and writhed. Imprisoning her mouth as his thumbs teased the tight, tender buds of her nipples, he effectively demolished resistance. Grievances forgotten, all she could concentrate on was the combination of sensations, the taste and smell and feel of him. The sand was warm. The morning sun blazed down from a deep blue sky. Fighting him suddenly didn't seem to be an option. Instead, ripples of desire surged through her, languorous and debilitating...

'Gaby...*Gaby*...' His throaty growl sent shivers down her spine. Mindlessly, she gazed at him through bewitched, lidded eyes as he stripped off her blouse and culottes, then his shorts and T-shirt, revealing skimpy navy boxer shorts and what seemed like acres of muscular, hair-coarsened brown body. 'I want to make love to you right here, right now...'

Disregarding her husky protest, he scooped her up in his arms and strode down to where the waters of the reefed lagoon lapped tranquilly against the white sand. The plunge into the water, sun-warmed though it was, briefly controlled the heat consuming her, but when he set her down, waist-deep in the ocean, and proceeded to slide the straps of her cream lace bra from her shoulders, and unclip the fastening, her eyes closed, and the invisible flames licked higher.

'Rick, this isn't the way...' she managed to croak, so helpless with longing that her voice sounded unrecognisable even to herself. 'Sex isn't the answer...'

'Maybe not, but it's never felt so good before, Gaby...' It was a half-laughing groan as he cupped her wet breasts in his hands, smoothing his thumbs compulsively, hungrily over the tight, hot peaks. 'I've lain awake ever since, *ma petite*, wanting you every second of every night, dying for you in my dreams...'

'In your *dreams*? Are you sure you weren't mixing me up with someone else?' she whispered, with a shaky attempt at levity, catching her breath in despair as he moved his hands lower. With a savage glitter in his eyes, he pushed down the scrap of lace panties, smoothing his hands possessively over the high, taut jut of her buttocks before lifting her slender hips in triumphant conquest against the masculine force of his body.

'There is no one else, you little cynic!' he rasped thickly in her ear. 'And I'm going to prove it to you, even if I have to lock you up here on my island...'

'Of all the arrogant, conceited things to——'

'Stop arguing,' he breathed roughly, moving against her with such explicit demand that all thought of argument disappeared from her head. 'Just let this happen, Gaby...'

Sensation took over, wild and hot and piercingly urgent. In an abrupt convulsion of need, she took his dark face in her hands, stroking unsteadily over the faint shadow on his jaw. He caught her little finger in his teeth, sucking on it with sensual teasing, and then she drove her fingers deep into the crisp spring of his hair, pulling his head against her breasts, offering herself with such total abandon that she hardly knew herself...

'All right,' she breathed with a shiver, 'I will... I can't help it, I want you so much...'

Nothing else mattered at that moment. The entire focus of her universe centred on this glorious, virile male, holding and trapping her in the strength of his arms.

'So sweet...so soft...' It was the bravura purr of a pirate. Cupping her small, tight buttocks in his palms, he lifted her higher, confidently, decisively, then drove deeply, irrevocably inside her, and as she cried out and clutched her arms fiercely around his neck, her legs around his waist, he waded slowly back to the shallows, sinking with powerful control to his knees as he closed up the last millimetre separating their bodies in a final, triumphant thrust of possession.

'You're mine, Gaby...' He shuddered the words against her lips, and with a choked cry of delight she arched helplessly against him. The need resonating through her lifted her into a realm of such astonishing pleasure that she could only cling to him like a drowning child. They were moving instinctively in the timeless rhythm of love, mouths, bodies, limbs frantically entwined, the sensations quivered, swelled, and expanded into such dizzying heat that she feared she might burn forever...

What felt like aeons later, she lifted herself on to her elbows in the warm, rippling shallows, and turned to look at Rick. Like a victorious bandit, he lay flat on his back, eyes closed, his magnificent physique glinting in the sun.

'That,' she accused softly, watching his amber eyes open a fraction and focus on her flushed face, 'was cheating!'

'Was it?' he murmured, his wide mouth twisting as he lifted his head to inspect her more closely. 'In this case, Gaby, the end justifies the means.'

'So cheating is all right, so long as it gets you what you want?' she confirmed huskily.

'*Mais oui, bien sûr!*' The grin he shot at her was irresistible. She was beginning to push herself to her feet, but he shot out a hand and caught hold of her arm, pulling her back down, the melting warmth in his eyes infinitely disturbing.

Self-consciousness seemed to have deserted her, she reflected dimly, as his gaze raked her naked body up and down in silent appreciation. She even summoned the courage to do likewise to him, heat suffusing her as she assimilated the power of his build, and the daunting masculinity of his physique. She received his devastating pirate's grin as her reward.

'Stay where you are,' he ordered softly. 'I claim full rights to all mermaids washed ashore on my island...'

'Rick!' He was so outrageous, she had to laugh. 'Has anyone ever offered you treatment for your dangerous power complex?'

'Never. They wouldn't dare.' His narrowed smile was contagious. 'Don't move, I'll be back...'

With blithe lack of inhibition, he waded back into the sea to retrieve their discarded underwear, nonchalantly pulled on his denim shorts, and then disappeared up the beach towards the house. Left in the sun, naked as a sea nymph, and, if she were totally truthful, lacking the energy to move,

Gabriella closed her eyes and wondered briefly about her own sanity...

She'd been overwhelmed and outmanoeuvred, but logically nothing had changed. At least she could make an effort at modesty. She could try to find a swimsuit from her suitcase, she decided dazedly. She'd just managed to rummage around and scramble into a skimpily cut, bright apricot Lycra one-piece when Rick was back. He was carrying sun-parasol, picnic rug, towels, and a coolbox.

'I assume I'm allowed to wear *clothes* during my enforced captivity?' she enquired with pointed irony.

'Only some of the time,' he teased huskily, grinning at the pinkening of her cheeks. 'And don't start lecturing me on my power complex again, Gaby. Come and have some lunch...'

It was extremely hard, she decided indignantly, to maintain the correct levels of cool uninterest and necessary suspicion, after being ravished in a tropical lagoon and then fed iced champagne and spicy prawns. A ravenous appetite didn't help.

'Hungry, Gaby?' Rick's deep voice held a wary note of humour. Tension was creeping into the outwardly idyllic scene.

'Incredibly,' she admitted, with a faint dimple of a smile, starting on the strawberries. 'It must be all this *abnormal* activity in the fresh air.'

'There is nothing abnormal about what we just did, Gaby.'

'Speak for yourself,' she informed him coolly, taking a fortifying sip of champagne, and sliding her legs out straight on the green checked rug. 'You probably make a habit of wild abandon on deserted beaches. I don't...'

'I know that.' The words were softly spoken, conveying such intimacy that embarrassed heat prickled her skin all over. Closing her eyes, Gabriella abruptly acknowledged her frightening vulnerability. When she opened them again, she met such glittering brilliance in Rick's lazy, lidded stare that she felt as if she'd been branded, all the way down to her soul...

'Gaby, will you listen to me?' The deep voice was compelling. Staring at him in silence for a moment, she found herself shrugging, with an attempt at being non-committal.

'OK.' She smiled with false brightness. 'Fire away. I'm all ears...'

'First, I'm sorry for not properly introducing myself. As Patrick St Josef, erstwhile photographer and averagely wealthy divorcee...'

'I expect I can live with that,' she quipped lightly. Casting her gaze around the beach near by, she spotted her discarded sunglasses and reached to retrieve them. She felt better defended, once they were back on.

'And next, I'm sorry for not telling you I was buying *First Flair* magazine. I couldn't be sure how closely you were in touch with Ursula. Until the take-over was confirmed by my financial advisers, Gaby, I couldn't risk anything getting back to her. It could have jeopardised the deal...'

'Fine. I can see your point of view.'

There was a cool silence following this glib, deliberately disinterested response.

'Finally...' Rick's voice had deepened, hardened '...that brings me to my relationship with Ursula——'

'Look, it's all right!' she burst out, suddenly trembling inside. 'You don't have to justify every past action! I've...I've realised something in this last half-hour or so. I've realised that physical feelings are...are somehow quite separate for men...'

'What in the name of hell are you talking about?'

'About being *naïve*, and immature!' she countered unsteadily. 'Instead of being...*sophisticated* and worldly-wise! I've just grown up!'

'You have?' The wry disbelief in his voice caught her on the raw.

'*Yes*! So I'm going to spare you all the...the turgid female emotional depths!' she ploughed on determinedly, her fingers nervously pleating the white towel on the sand beside her. 'I accept that what we just did felt good. It was good. Just like the first time you made love to me. That felt...good too...'

'Good?' The echo was a mocking taunt.

'Yes. So you can stop all these soul-searching explanations, and feelings of guilt and...and obligation...'

'Ah, I think I'm beginning to see...' The dark gleam in Rick's amber eyes was unsettling. 'What you're saying is, "Thanks for the great sex, and we can part as friends"?'

'Yes...' The twist of anguish caught at her stomach without warning, and she clenched her fingers into the towel, nodding calmly. 'Yes,' she repeated a fraction doubtfully, a small catch in her throat betraying her. 'That's exactly what I'm saying...!'

Rick's steady gaze was suddenly grim, the laughter gone. After what felt like an eternity, he said slowly, 'I don't believe I'm hearing this. This is what I'm getting from the delectable little virgin I've fallen half crazy in love with, some sickening line in worldly-wise sophistry?'

'Don't patronise me, Rick, I...' She stopped uncertainly, his words sinking home. 'What did you say?' It was a shaky whisper, and she despised herself for her emotional devastation.

'*Ecoute-moi bien*, Gabriella,' he chided harshly, coming over to sit disturbingly close behind her on the rug, pulling her back against the heat of his body. She trembled convulsively at the intimacy he'd created, and he stroked long, strong fingers over the sensitive nape of her neck beneath her hair, then caught her head between his hands and turned her face round, removing the sunglasses again as he looked into her eyes. The kindling glow in the golden gaze turned her limbs to water. 'Pay attention, please. *Je t'aime. Je t'aime*! *Tu comprends*? I love you. Believe it or not, *mignonne*, I fell in love with you the very first second I saw you. I just couldn't accept it was possible...'

'Rick, what about——?'

'*Tais toi*, Gabriella!' he ground out, sliding his hands down to the small indentations above her collarbones, clasping her shoulders gently and giving her a slight shake. 'After my marriage went wrong, I'd sworn I'd never make myself vulnerable again. Suddenly, nine years on, I was looking at the only girl I wanted to spend my life with, and it didn't make any sense! Particularly since she appeared to have labelled me a worthless philanderer to rival the last man in her life. I fought the crazy feeling as long as I could——'

'But Rick——'

'Why do you think I agreed to bring you across here with that cyclone building up?' he persisted, ignoring her husky interruption. 'Didn't you guess that I must have taken a calculated risk, just to give myself some time with you?'

'You *did* ... ?'

'I freely confess to the crime,' he murmured drily. 'And then you went down with flu, and began to ramble deliriously about this cursed Piers...'

'Oh, Rick——'

'Be quiet. Let me finish. That's why, when I found you were a virgin, *ma petite*, I could not bring myself to take advantage of you. I thought you must still be in love with this Piers. That you must have been...saving yourself for him. That's why I told you I wasn't interested, when I'd have given my life at that moment to make love to you!'

'I just didn't feel the right way about him,' she said in a low, shaky voice. Rick's nearness, the muscular strength of his hard body encircling hers from behind, was sending *frissons* of response skittering up and down her spine and along every nerve-ending. 'He...he even tried to force me, one night...before I gave him back his ring.'

'Then I will personally wring the little bastard's neck,' Rick stated flatly, a note of such steely anger in his voice that she felt a momentary stab of dismay.

'No need...' she said with a slight laugh. 'I—er—wounded him in a slightly indelicate part of his anatomy in self-defence...'

'Did you indeed?' Rick sounded huskily amused. 'I can't tell you how pleased I am to hear it! Before I knew this, I was gratified that my bid for *First Flair* had beaten that of the Wellington Group. Now, I have an even greater satisfaction, *mignonne*.'

'Sadist!'

'No. I am not a sadist, Gaby,' he teased softly. 'But neither am I an angel. I lied about the radio being damaged,' he told her, with a flash of a grin as she twisted her head up to frown at him. 'It wasn't damaged. I just wanted a little more time, to work out how you felt, how I felt...'

Gabriella felt as if some invisible power supply had switched on inside her, lighting up every dark corner and crevice, making her glow from within, radiant as a floodlight. But she stared round at Rick's dark, intense face behind hers as if she were seeing him for the first time.

'You mean... all that time we could have radioed the marina to be rescued?' she affirmed, in mounting astonishment.

He inclined his dark head, watching her intently through narrowed, darkening eyes.

'And... Ursula...?' she ventured finally, beginning to drown in the possessive gleam of his gaze.

'Ursula is a conniving bitch,' he said succinctly, his mouth twisting ruefully. 'I have never, I swear to you in total honesty, never made love to Ursula Taylor. We've worked together on and off for years. She's made it clear that she would welcome a little...extra-marital diversion. That's not my style, and it never has been. The Taylors' marriage has been on the rocks for years, but it had nothing to do with me. God knows what she told her husband, but the divorce citation was the last straw. That's what we "disagreed" about, Gaby. That's why I told her I would never work with her again. And that's why she has been stirring up as much trouble as she can...'

Wide-eyed, she searched the dark face above her. Her heart was beginning to thump unevenly. Her nervous system felt shredded.

'I love you, Rick,' she whispered simply. 'With or without your power complex.'

'I know you do,' he grinned, crossing and tightening his arms over her chest to enfold her completely as she wriggled indignantly. 'You told me so, that unforgettable night, Gaby, when you bravely ripped your T-shirt off and made me a gift of your body...'

'You're...*incorrigible*! So arrogant...!'

With a hoarse laugh, he buried his face in her damp blonde hair, and in spite of herself she began to laugh with him.

'Marry me?' he whispered into her hair, his hands moving intimately over the jut of her breasts beneath the tight apricot Lycra. 'Soon, Gaby?'

'*Marry* you?' she breathed unsteadily.

'What else?' Sliding his hands to her neck, he ran his fingers up into her hair, cupped her head between his hands, and she caught his hands and covered them tightly with her own. Twisting her mouth round blindly, she kissed his fingers, closing her eyes with a shudder of happiness so intense that it frightened her...

'I told you,' he said, his voice deepening and thickening, 'I want everything from you. In return you have everything from me. Including my heart, always. But I want you as my wife, Gaby.'

She drew a shaky breath, and her eyes were very bright green as she met his gaze.

'You just want to keep up with your ancestors—you want a conveniently imported wife,' she teased unsteadily. 'Some biddable, duty-free female you've rounded up to colonise this exclusive little island of yours.'

'A *biddable* female?' he echoed teasingly, twisting her round in his arms to bring her into full contact with the hard warmth of his body. 'Then in your case my judgement must be sadly impaired, *chérie*! Perhaps you meant "beddable"?'

With a muffled shriek, she tried to thump him and was flattened on the rug for her pains.

'A duty-free imported wife sounds a fair deal, however,' he taunted outrageously, moving his mouth in an inflammatory fashion against her lips. 'Let me see—how many children will we need to have, to found a new St Josef dynasty, Gaby?'

'Quite a few,' she laughed. She felt helpless with happiness as she pulled his head down and kissed him. 'I've always wanted lots of children, so that's no problem. But if we're founding a dynasty,' she added, huskily, 'there's no time to waste, wouldn't you say...?'

'I would agree, *ma chérie*.' His amber gaze was brilliant with teasing laughter as he crushed her triumphantly into the hard warmth of his arms, desire rekindling between them. 'We have absolutely no time to waste at all...!'

Next Month's Romances

Each month you can choose from a wide variety of romance with Mills & Boon. Below are the new titles to look out for next month, why not ask either Mills & Boon Reader Service or your Newsagent to reserve you a copy of the titles you want to buy – just tick the titles you would like and either post to Reader Service or take it to any Newsagent and ask them to order your books.

Please save me the following titles: Please tick	✓

Title	Author	
ENEMY WITHIN	Amanda Browning	
THE COLOUR OF MIDNIGHT	Robyn Donald	
VAMPIRE LOVER	Charlotte Lamb	
STRANGE INTIMACY	Anne Mather	
SUMMER OF THE STORM	Catherine George	
ICE AT HEART	Sophie Weston	
OUTBACK TEMPTATION	Valerie Parv	
DIVIDED BY LOVE	Kathryn Ross	
DARK SIDE OF THE ISLAND	Edwina Shore	
IN THE HEAT OF PASSION	Sara Wood	
SHADOW OF A TIGER	Jane Donnelly	
BEWARE A LOVER'S LIE	Stephanie Howard	
PASSIONATE OBSESSION	Christine Greig	
SWEET MADNESS	Sharon Kendrick	
STRANGER AT THE WEDDING	Joan Mary Hart	
VALERIE	Debbie Macomber	
OBLIGATION TO LOVE	Catherine O'Connor	

If you would like to order these books in addition to your regular subscription from Mills & Boon Reader Service please send £1.90 per title to: Mills & Boon Reader Service, Freepost, P.O. Box 236, Croydon, Surrey, CR9 9EL, quote your Subscriber No:.................................. (If applicable) and complete the name and address details below. Alternatively, these books are available from many local Newsagents including W H Smith, J Menzies, Martins and other paperback stockists from 10 June 1994.

Name:...

Address:...

....Post Code:...........................

To Retailer: If you would like to stock M&B books please contact your regular book/magazine wholesaler for details.

You may be mailed with offers from other reputable companies as a result of this application. If you would rather not take advantage of these opportunities please tick box ☐

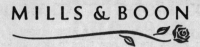

MILLS & BOON

Proudly present...

CHARLOTTE LAMB'S
♥ *100th* ♥
ROMANCE

This is a remarkable achievement for a writer who had her first Mills & Boon novel published in 1973. Some six million words later and with sales around the world, her novels continue to be popular with romance fans everywhere.

Her centenary romance '*VAMPIRE LOVER*' is a suspense-filled story of dark desires and tangled emotions—Charlotte Lamb at her very best.

Published: June 1994   **Price: £1.90**

Accept 4 FREE Romances and 2 FREE gifts

FROM READER SERVICE

Here's an irresistible invitation from Mills & Boon. Please accept our offer of 4 FREE Romances, a CUDDLY TEDDY and a special MYSTERY GIFT! Then, if you choose, go on to enjoy 6 captivating Romances every month for just £1.90 each, postage and packing FREE. Plus our FREE Newsletter with author news, competitions and much more.

Send the coupon below to:
Mills & Boon Reader Service,
FREEPOST, PO Box 236,
Croydon, Surrey CR9 9EL.

NO STAMP REQUIRED

Yes! Please rush me 4 FREE Romances and 2 FREE gifts! Please also reserve me a Reader Service subscription. If I decide to subscribe I can look forward to receiving 6 brand new Romances for just £11.40 each month, post and packing FREE. If I decide not to subscribe I shall write to you within 10 days - I can keep the free books and gifts whatever I choose. I may cancel or suspend my subscription at any time. I am over 18 years of age.

Ms/Mrs/Miss/Mr _____ EP70R

Address _____

_____

Postcode _____ Signature _____

mps
MAILING
PREFERENCE
SERVICE